DATE DUE

The Ghost Squad and the Halloween Conspiracy

By the Same Author

The Ghost Squad and the Halloween Conspiracy

by E. W. Hildick

A Ghost Squad Book

E. P. DUTTON   NEW YORK

To Jock Sanderson,
who put me in touch

LIBRARY OF CONGRESS CATALOGING IN PUBLICATION DATA

Hildick, E. W. (Edmund Wallace), date.
　The Ghost Squad and the Halloween conspiracy.
　(A Ghost Squad book)
　Summary: Four young ghosts uncover a plot by a
senator's stepson to have his stepfather unwittingly pass out
candy with embedded needles at a Halloween party.
　　1. Children's stories, American. [1. Ghosts—Fiction.
2. Halloween—Fiction. 3. Mystery and detective
stories] I. Title. II. Series: Hildick, E. W. (Edmund
Wallace), date. Ghost Squad book.
PZ7.H5463Gg 1985 [Fic] 85-6835
ISBN 0-525-44111-5

Published in the United States by E. P. Dutton,
2 Park Avenue, New York, N.Y. 10016

Published simultaneously in Canada by
Fitzhenry & Whiteside Limited, Toronto

Editor: Julie Amper

Printed in the U.S.A.　　COBE　　First Edition
10 9 8 7 6 5 4 3 2 1

Contents

1
The Needles

"Hey! Look! What is he *doing?*"

The speaker was a tall blond girl of about sixteen, dressed in white shorts and a red shirt. She was standing on the patio at the back of a large rambling house, and she was peering through a sliding glass door, her face up close to it.

Her three companions turned. They'd all been busy with their search, stooping to the low terrace walls that bordered the patio, looking into various cracks and corners and the tubs and troughs that still held clumps of the hardier plants left over from summer.

The oldest member of the group frowned as he straightened up.

"Never mind what somebody's doing *inside* the house, Karen. We're here to look for a wallet that was lost outside, not to snoop into people's private affairs."

He was tall, with broad shoulders and red hair. Across the front of his T-shirt, the words ARMSTRONG CONSTRUCTION began to fold up into creases as he bent once more to his task.

"Joe's right, Karen!" said one of the others. "For Pete's sake, don't waste your energy. You know what an extra drain it can be if you use it for that kinda thing. And we still have the rest of the grounds to search, all the way down to the main gate."

The boy who said this was about thirteen. He had dark shaggy hair and bright eyes. He too wore a T-shirt with a logo: a wheel with the large letter *G* in the center and letters of the alphabet and other symbols at the end of the spokes. But he never paused in his search for more than a couple of seconds—bending and dipping and darting from clump to clump, making the letters and symbols seem to dance and spin.

"I know that, Carlos!" said the girl, turning her head briefly and causing her long blond hair to fly. "But this *isn't* snooping! This is serious. This looks much more important than searching for the wallet. . . . Right, Danny? What do *you* think? I mean, look—just look at the guy!"

The fourth member of the group was already staring into the room. His eyes bulged from his pale thin face. His normally anxious expression began to curl and harden into one of horror.

"Hey!" he said, in a croaky whisper. "Are—are those *needles* he's sticking into the candy?"

His narrow shoulders hunched higher in his black imitation-leather windbreaker as he cupped his hands at either side of his eyes, to focus better on the sinister pile of sharp metal objects on the table inside.

"Needles?" said Joe Armstrong, suddenly arrested.

"In *candy?*" said Carlos Gomez, abandoning his search and darting up to the window. "Gosh! Yeah! He's *spiking* that candy. They're old phonograph needles. And—and—some of them look rusty!"

"And only two days from Halloween!" said Karen. "Hey, Joe! Come and take a look."

But Joe was already there, staring in.

"You're right," he murmured. His mouth was stretched in a grim line. "He's doing a very careful job, too. And—uh—just look at the expression on his face!"

The young man sitting at the table facing the sliding door and glancing up at it from time to time was fairly good-looking. His black hair was thick but well groomed. He had a firm chin, a straight nose and deep blue eyes with long lashes. His mouth was broad and generous, and a faint smile was playing at its corners as he got on with his work—deftly unwrapping the gold foil on the bars of chocolate, pressing in the needles so that there was nothing of them showing and then delicately brushing with a gloved thumb and finger the places the needles had pierced.

Considering the nature of his task, the pleasant smile was horrible, transforming every other good thing about his features into something false and evil.

"Who is the creep, anyway?" said Carlos.

"Vinnie Boyars," said Joe. "The senator's stepson. When his mother married the senator about ten years ago, she had Vinnie take the same name—and he hates it. I always knew he was a jerk, but I never thought he'd stoop to *this.*"

"Who does he intend to give them to, I wonder?"

said Karen, shuddering at the thought of young delicate lips and gums and tongues and throats closing around that chocolate, champing down on it. . . .

"Looks like he's getting it ready for a whole *bunch* of kids," said Carlos. "A whole—hey!" He broke off, wide-eyed. "Don't tell me he—"

Then he broke off again.

"Someone's coming," said Joe, turning to look toward the corner of the patio.

The sound of footsteps on the graveled walk at the side of the house was getting louder. So was a pattering, jingling noise.

"Let's hope whoever it is catches the creep at his dirty work," said Karen.

"*He's* heard the sounds, too," said Danny. "Look."

Vinnie had started up, alert and narrow-eyed. He was throwing a large cloth over the piles of chocolate bars and needles.

Then the newcomers rounded the corner: a young woman with a fully grown, rather fat golden retriever on a chain.

The dog suddenly gave a strangled yelp as it strained toward the door. At the sound of it, the man inside seemed to relax a little. His grin broadened.

"Hi!" he said, as the woman reached the door. "Come on in! It's open."

The group of watchers had parted to give the woman access. She took no notice of them, but this wasn't merely because she only had eyes for the handsome Vinnie. *He* wasn't taking any notice of them, either, any more than he had done earlier, when he was busy with his furtive task and they'd been standing there

4

in a row, staring at him with looks of horror and dis-gust on their faces.

In fact, only the dog paid any attention to them. It cringed and whimpered and broke into feeble snarls as the woman tugged at the chain to lead it past them.

And that was because it was one of the very few animals that are able to see ghosts.

2
The Conspiracy

There was a partly open window at the side of the sliding door. When the woman and the dog had stepped into the room and she had closed the door firmly behind her, the four ghosts moved over to the window.

"That's better," said Joe. "Now maybe we'll be able to *hear* what this is all about."

"We shoulda moved in quick, while she had the door open," said Carlos.

"There wouldn't have been time for us all to slip through," said Karen. "She's in too much of a hurry. Look at her. *Throwing* herself at him!"

The woman had walked straight up to Vinnie, eagerly, lips puckering, arms out.

But Vinnie neatly sidestepped.

"Not now, Jeanine. I'm busy."

Jeanine was about the same age as Joe, twenty-two

or twenty-three, and a couple of years older than Vinnie. At first, as she crossed the room—all girlish and giggly—she'd seemed the younger of the two. But when Vinnie brushed her aside, her rather plump face tightened under its layers of makeup, accentuating the frown lines, and then she looked her age. She was wearing a black turtleneck sweater, tight jeans and lots of gold: a large ring that held her pulled-back mousy brown hair in a ponytail, a thick necklace and pendant and several bracelets. She let her arms drop and her shoulders slump, and the gold, which up until then had been dancing and jingling, fell silent.

Vinnie gave her a quick sly glance. The corners of his mouth twitched. He seemed to relish her disappointment. She pouted angrily.

"Oh? Busy on what?"

Vinnie's grin quivered again. A dimple in the center of his chin deepened.

"Preparing treats," he said. "With a trick or two inside them."

He whipped off the cloth. The woman stared at the gold-wrapped bars, with their bright red lettering. Then at the pile of needles.

"Treats? Tricks?" Then her eyes widened. "What—what are you *doing*, Vinnie?"

Those last few words were pretty much the same as those uttered by Karen, earlier. But there was a world of difference in their tone. Karen's had lifted on a rising note of horror. Jeanine's went up with a lilt of gleeful anticipation.

"She sounds as bad as *him!*" Karen cried out.

The dog, which had settled uneasily under the table, lifted its head and growled at the window.

7

"What's with the dog?" said Vinnie, bending to look at it, his eyebrows meeting with annoyance.

"Quiet, Dana!" Jeanine said hurriedly. "It's some animal outside, I guess. She must have picked up its scent or something."

"There's nobody else out there, is there?"

"Of course not. I'd have seen, wouldn't I?" She went to the window and seemed to peer straight into the four faces, one at a time. "No. Not a soul." She turned. "But this chocolate . . . those needles. What's it all about? You aren't *really* going to give them to somebody, are you?"

Vinnie was openly grinning now. His eyes had a bright glint in them—too bright, slightly mad.

"Me? Give somebody spiked candy? You must be kidding. As if I'd ever do such a thing!"

"Well—"

The woman was smiling doubtfully.

"No. Big Daddy's gonna do that," said Vinnie. "Big Step-Daddy. State Senator Everett Boyars, 'The Children's Senator.' *That's* who'll be giving the spiked candy to the kids!"

"But—I don't understand—I thought—"

"You want to hear about my plan or not?" snapped Vinnie.

Jeanine got very quiet then.

They all did.

Even the dog.

Vinnie started his explanation slowly, as if he was reluctant to go into what *he* considered painful details. His mouth took on a bitter twist and his forehead wrinkled up like a querulous little kid's. Once or twice at this stage, Jeanine seemed about to reach out and pat his hand, but she must have thought better of it. Vinnie's eyes still had an ugly glitter.

"I mean, you know how it is between me and him. Like he's always had a grudge against me, just for being *me*. Like he's always glad of the chance to preach at me. 'Mend your ways, son. Stop fooling around. Settle down to some work, for a change.' . . . Yuck!"

Vinnie glared around.

"I mean, half the money he's got is what Mom left him when she died. So whose money is it, huh? Tell me *that!*"

His voice had risen to a whine. The dog growled. Jeanine put a gentle, cautious foot on its back, and it lowered its head again. Vinnie seemed not to have heard.

"Anyway, when I got kicked out of college last year, and he cut my allowance in half and said he wouldn't restore it until I'd *proved* myself—*proved* myself!—that did it. I vowed I'd bring him down off his pedestal, his pulpit, and let *him* have a taste of what it's like when everyone's against you. Maybe it would make him loosen up a bit, including his purse strings."

Vinnie's upper lip curled—part sneer, part snarl.

"I mean, *him*—setting himself up as the young people's friend, holding out a helping hand to all kindsa delinquents and riff-raff, as long as they're under eighteen and he gets full publicity! Well, I'm gonna hit him just where it'll hurt most!"

His eyes were glowing as he toyed with one of the doctored bars.

"You know how I got the idea?"

The woman shook her head, staring at the gloved

fingers. She seemed in danger of being hypnotized.

"I heard him talking on the phone to one of his old delinquents," said Vinnie. "Dino Gorusso. You know who I mean?"

"Sure. Dino's Discounts. That store on Railroad Street. I didn't know *he'd* ever been in trouble, though."

"Plenty. Five, six years ago. I know all about it. Boy, don't I ever! Isn't the old fool always ramming it down my throat? 'Look at Dino Gorusso,' he keeps saying. 'He was wild too, when he was a kid. But look at him now, after he straightened himself out. One of the wealthiest store-owners in town, and still only in his twenties.' Ha!"

Vinnie took time out to think about this. With deep hatred, judging from the look on his face.

"That guy is poison!" murmured Joe. "Pure poison!"

"Looks crazy, to me," said Danny.

"That also," grunted Joe. "But mainly poison."

The woman coughed.

"Uh—the phone call, Vinnie. You were saying—"

"Yeah." Vinnie gave his head a brisk shake. He dropped the chocolate bar back on the table. "Well, I didn't pay too much attention to it at the time, a few weeks ago. Except that it did sound sort of strange. Like making a fuss out of nothing." Vinnie shrugged. "But that's the senator's style, anyway."

"*Strange*, though?"

"Yeah. Something like—'Yes, Dino. Candy. That's right. Candy. But it has to be very special. And, Dino'—these words I remember exactly—'it has to be very confidential. OK?' "

10

Vinnie grinned.

"I picked up on *that* word, all right! But before I could hear any more, Josephine came schlepping along the corridor and I had to move away from his door. . . . Anyway, I'd nearly forgotten about it until just a few days ago. When I found his wallet."

This caused a stir among the four outside listeners. The one inside raised her head.

"*You* found it? The one he's been advertising a reward for?"

"Yeah. The one he dropped when he was out jogging. He thought he must have lost it someplace between the main gate and the old covered bridge. The dumb old cluck thought *he'd* covered the grounds themselves thoroughly, when he searched later. What he didn't know was that I'd spotted it even before he knew it was missing. Out there on the lawn."

The ghosts looked at one another.

"Told you!" whispered Carlos.

"And you didn't hand it over?" said Jeanine.

"Naw! Why should I? Old cheapskate, with his lousy twenty-dollar reward! And all those credit cards." Vinnie frowned. "Not much cash, though, worse luck." Then he brightened. "But who cares? That's where I found the sales slip."

"What sales slip?"

"Dino's Discounts. Itemizing one hundred chocolate bars. Dino's price: sixty dollars. Genuine Belgian chocolate and worth more than twice that amount."

"These?"

"Yeah. It was the word *Belgian* that did it. Dino had

even written it on the slip, like he was proud to give his old buddy just what he'd asked for. And then I knew what it was all about."

"What?"

Vinnie leered at his visitor.

"Well," he said, tantalizingly. "Think. Where is the great Senator Boyars now?"

"How should I know?"

"Don't you ever read the papers? Oh, never mind! . . . He's in *Belgium*, of course. Big children's welfare conference in Brussels. And he'll be flying back on Saturday, leaving the conference early, racing back so he doesn't miss the Halloween party he's throwing here."

"Halloween—?"

"Every year. Always a bunch of underprivileged kids. Orphans and whatnot. And always with a TV crew and reporters present. To take pictures of Big Daddy throwing his corny scared act. Then dishing out the treats."

"You mean—?"

"I mean what is he giving them for treats *this* year? Why, these lovely expensive Belgian chocolate bars that he's taken the trouble to buy over there and bring all the way back here. What else? That way, he makes sure his *trip* gets full publicity, too."

"But you just said he bought them from Dino."

"Sure! But that isn't what he'll tell the reporters. That's why it had to be so confidential. Don't you see that? . . . Anyway, as soon as I saw that slip I realized he'd actually bought the bars, ready. And I also knew for what. And, knowing that—that he had them already stashed—naturally I knew where to look for them."

"Where?"

"His den, dummy! Where else? He has a closet in there. He calls it his Hospitality Closet. Where he keeps his special drinks and stuff. It's always locked, but that doesn't faze me. I know exactly where he hides the key. And—sure as your name's Jeanine Zimmerman—the chocolate bars were in there."

"These?"

"Yeah!" Vinnie was chuckling now, really enjoying his story. "To be handed out in front of the TV cameras. Jolly old senator dishes out his treats. Kids start taking bites. Yummy, yummy! . . . Then the yells and screams and the blood, all mixed with melted chocolate."

The woman was staring fascinated at Vinnie's dimple. A slow grin began to spread on her face.

Karen nearly flipped.

"Look! Look at her now! She's as rotten and crazy as he is!"

Then the woman frowned.

"But Vinnie, dear, no one will ever believe that the senator put the needles in."

Vinnie gave a weird kind of giggle, almost hugging himself with glee.

"No, but the shock and the shame will be there. The shock that he could be so careless. And—and so *cheap*. Buying them off an ex-crook and trying to make out that he took more time and went to more trouble and expense than he did! Because, naturally, there'll be an investigation. And that'll lead direct to Dino.

Then *he'll* be under suspicion. Hey! It's beautiful! Two birds with one stone!"

"But what about *you*, Vinnie? Won't you be a suspect?"

"Me? Why?" The look of innocence on Vinnie's face just then was the most chilling expression he'd worn that afternoon. The most chilling of a very chilling bunch. "*I'm* not supposed to know about his deal with Dino. That was *confidential*, wasn't it? I'm not even supposed to know how to get into that closet. I'm always careful to top up the bottles with water—the bottles I sneak drinks from. Also—" The innocent expression faded. It was replaced by a cunning leer. "Look at these. See this? And this? And this?"

He was touching various bars.

"Yes. But—"

"So you see these small tears in the wrappers? I put them there." He unwrapped one of them. "Watch this," he said.

With the leer broadening, he bent down and handed the bar to the dog.

"No!" screamed the woman, attempting to snatch it from the dog's drooling jaws.

But Vinnie had her pinned by the arms.

"It's OK—look!" he said, as Dana champed appreciatively on the chocolate. "The ones with the torn wrappers are the bars that *don't* have needles in them. And old Vinnie's gonna be at that party, too, munching chocolate with the rest of them. And would *he* be eating it if he knew some of the bars were spiked? No way!" He laughed. "Besides," he went on, "I have one more ace up my sleeve. Or, rather, one more jack."

"What?"

The woman still hadn't recovered from the shock. Her face had turned a bluish white, and she was having difficulty controlling her breathing. The dog, sensing that something was wrong, had gone to stand by her side, whimpering up at her, then snarling softly at Vinnie through its chocolate-smeared jaws.

"It—it's all right, Dana," murmured the woman. "Sit! . . . Go on, Vinnie. What—what card do you have up your sleeve?"

"Not *what*, honey. *Who*. I'm talking about that grandson of Josephine's."

Suddenly, his companion looked around, at the open door behind them.

"Oh, it's OK," said Vinnie. "It's her afternoon off. She's gone to meet the kid after school. Taking him to a movie. *He's* my trump card. Anyone asks—I mean, if it really looks like someone is beginning to suspect me—I'm gonna drop it out, nice and casually, that— 'Hey! Wow! Yeah! Now I come to think of it, I did see Lester come out of the senator's den, one afternoon when he was supposed to be helping Josephine.' "

"Lester?" gasped Danny. "Is he talking about Lester Cartwright? That's Wacko's cousin, isn't it?"

"Sure is," said Carlos, gravely.

"This," said Karen, "is definitely a case for the full Ghost Squad!"

"Yeah!" grunted Joe, with a last worried look at the temptingly glittering candy bars and the menacingly glittering needles near them. "Let's go and contact the other two. Right now!"

3
The Great Ghost Debate

"Ghosts *can't* walk through walls. Or through any other solid substance."

The speaker was Henry Williams, known to his school friends and others as Wacko. He was a thin, frail-looking black kid, fifteen years old, with wide serious eyes that looked wider and more serious than ever as he made the statement. He was standing on the platform in the auditorium, where the after-school Debating Club's latest session was in full swing.

The audience stirred. Some laughed. Some murmured. There was a bigger attendance than usual. This was partly because of the nature of the subject, coming at that time of the year, and partly because during the past hour word had gotten around that this was something special, and kids from other clubs had started drifting in.

16

The motion was: This House Does Not Believe in Ghosts.

For the motion, the speakers were Tessa Grunwald and Dwayne Thompson, both of them bright, well-informed debaters. Against it were Wacko Williams and his friend, Buzz Phillips.

The last two weren't regular debaters. Wacko was much too scientifically minded, and most of his spare time was spent in his room at home, which was more like an electronics lab. Buzz was not quite so surprising a choice (or volunteer). In the last four or five months, he'd become close friends with Wacko and seemed to have been bitten by the electronics bug himself. He was also a pretty able speaker, especially on subjects he felt strongly about. So it seemed only natural that when Wacko volunteered so eagerly to oppose the motion, Buzz should be ready to back him up.

Also—and during the debate, quite a few members of the audience had found themselves remembering this—Buzz did have a certain prior connection with supernatural subjects. Hadn't his former best friend—Danny Green, killed in an accident earlier in the year—claimed to be able to dream about the future, with Buzz as his enthusiastic interpreter?

Tessa Grunwald pounced on Wacko's statement. With a quick triumphant glance at the audience through her large round glasses, she flicked out the tip of her tongue like a lizard snapping up a fly.

"Hey!" she said. "Just a second! Would you repeat that for me, please? You're now saying that these—

uh—supernatural bodies you believe in *cannot* walk through walls?"

Mr. Holly and Miss Perrins, the English teachers presiding over the meeting, looked at each other and shrugged. But they were also smiling. The debate had long since run off the formal rails and had developed into a rough and ready question-and-answer type of session. More like a courtroom scene really. But since everybody was so raptly interested, what did the stuffy old rules matter?

"Yes, I am saying that," said Wacko, and at his side Buzz Phillips nodded firmly.

Buzz was taller and burlier than Wacko, even though he was a year younger. He had a wide mouth and deep-set brown eyes. There was usually a smile on his mouth, but it was in a firm serious line now.

"And that includes closed doors and windows?" said Tessa, after flicking out her tongue again and flashing another "now-get-this" glance at her supporters in the audience.

Wacko nodded.

"That includes doors and windows. All solid barriers. Even screens."

"And he can say *that* again!" grumbled Carlos Gomez, Wacko's former best friend, shuffling about impatiently in the space in front of the platform, where he and the other three had finally managed to work their way.

After all, they had just had to wait nearly fifteen minutes for someone to open the auditorium main door long enough for them to be able to slip through!

Tessa glanced at her seconder, to see if Dwayne Thompson had any follow-up. Dwayne, a thin-faced hungry-looking kid, certainly had. He nodded quickly and took up the questioning.

"Leaving aside the question of solids and supernatural invisible beings for a moment—though it beats me that anything *so* insubstantial can't go through whatever barrier it wants—"

"Oh, yeah?" Buzz interrupted. "So how about the wind? Huh? Who can see the wind? Yet the wind can't go through solid objects, can it?"

A cheer rose from the audience. A good number of these kids really *wanted* to believe in ghosts.

"Order!" shouted Mr. Holly. Then he turned. "Continue, Dwayne."

Dwayne had been looking rather lost for an answer to Buzz's counter-question. But, being a good debater, he shrugged it off and went on with his own main question.

"You see, what puzzles me is this. If there *were* such things as ghosts, if everybody becomes a ghost when they die, and if you take into account the vast number of people who've lived and died on this planet ever since it was created—well, then, wouldn't there be wall-to-wall ghosts everywhere? I mean jam-packed together and stacked in layers miles high? It seems to me they'd have no room to haunt anybody. No freedom of movement even to flap their arms the way they're supposed to, let alone go through doors."

This time the cheers came from the antighost section. Even some of Buzz and Wacko's supporters were beginning to look doubtful.

Wacko's eyes flashed.

"In the first place, they do *not* flap their arms around like that," he said.

"But more important than that," said Buzz, "is you've got it all wrong. Everybody does *not* become a ghost."

This caused a stir. Tessa's tongue flicked out three times in quick succession.

"Say again?" she drawled, head on one side, nose all wrinkled up, like she couldn't believe her ears.

"Everybody does *not* become a ghost," Buzz repeated. "It's a very selective process."

By now, the four ghosts themselves were up on the platform.

"Where do they get all this from?" they heard Mr. Holly whisper as he glanced uneasily at Buzz and Wacko. "They seem so *sure* of their facts."

"Robert Phillips is a very imaginative boy," murmured Miss Perrins, smiling approvingly at her favorite student.

"I wish they'd fudge their facts more!" Joe muttered.

"Why?" said Karen. "They're doing just fine."

"They're doing *too* fine. Right, Joe?" said Danny.

"Yeah! They'll give away too many secrets if they're not careful."

"Also," said Carlos, flicking his fingers with impatience, "they could go on for hours—hours and hours and hours—and we have to tell them about this conspiracy."

But for a while it seemed as if nothing could stop the two friends. Buzz and Wacko felt challenged. They also knew that they had more than enough firsthand information to absolutely bury the challengers.

And when Tessa said, with a slight sneer, "Who

does get to be a ghost, then?"—Joe groaned. He could see what was coming.

"First," said Buzz, firmly and confidently, beginning to tick off the items on his fingers, "first and most important of all, those people with strong loving links to the survivors."

"Survivors like friends and relatives who grieve *too* much," said Wacko. "Who're taking it too hard. Who may be in trouble. Who were used to getting lots of help from the dead person."

"Who feel lost without the dead person," said Buzz.

There was a hush in the entire auditorium now. Tessa's tongue came out, but it was only to lick her lips nervously. Miss Perrins sniffed loudly and began to dab at her nose with a handkerchief.

"Oh, boy!" murmured Karen.

"So these ghosts hang around, hoping to be able to comfort the survivors," said Buzz. "And they're usually pretty miserable, because there isn't much they can do now, is there?"

"Anyway," Wacko quickly cut in, as if he'd realized where this might lead them if they went into too much detail, "in time, when the grief of the living dies down, the ghosts connected with them move on, fade out, pass away again."

"All of which is speeded up in the case of main category number two," said Buzz, ticking off his second finger. "Which is a good thing, because this kind of ghost is bound to earth by strong *hating* links."

A few of the younger listeners began to squirm with pleasure. This was the kind of ghost *they'd* heard about.

"This kind," said Wacko, "hangs around hoping to do harm to their old enemies. And because *these* ghosts can't do much about it, either—even though they see so many opportunities, now that they're invisible and can go almost anywhere—*they* get mad."

"Madder and madder," agreed Buzz. "So that they quickly burn themselves out, trying to get revenge without any easy way of bringing it off."

Some of the kids laughed, gleeful at the hating ghosts' big problem. Then their laughter faded when Buzz, looking stern, added:

"Though there *could* be ways, of course. Ways a really clever Mal—a really smart malevolent ghost can do harm indirectly." His voice dropped. The audience craned forward. "You never know with ghosts."

"The bum!" howled Carlos. "He's beginning to enjoy all this attention! He's hamming it up!"

"But you see what this means," said Wacko, in a drier, more scientific tone than Buzz's. "It means that very few very *old* people ever stay behind as ghosts. Their loves and their hates have usually faded out while they were alive. Even if they have anyone left alive to love or hate."

That calmed the audience down some, making them more thoughtful. Then Buzz had to go and stir them up again.

"But there *are* very old ghosts," he said. "Old in their—uh—ghosthood, I mean. They may be young-*looking*, if they died young, but this category can sometimes hang around for centuries."

"Oh, yeah?" said Dwayne.

"Yes," said Buzz. "These are the ghosts of people who, when they were alive, were more attached to places than to people. Old beautiful houses or castles they'd grown up in. Or churches or cathedrals or abbeys, if they were monks or priests. Or even particular stretches of countryside."

"Sure," said Wacko, "but they only hang around while those places, or the ruins of those places, remain. Or the countryside stays as it used to be in their time."

"Which is why," said Buzz, "old, old buildings, or very remote unspoiled places, can give living visitors a spooky feeling."

"He's even giving *me* a spooky feeling!" said Carlos. "I wish he'd wrap it up, though."

"And finally," said Wacko, as if he'd heard his old friend, "there is one category of person who *never* becomes a ghost."

Tessa sighed. She knew when she was licked. These guys had prepared their case too well. Inventing all these crazy details!

"Go on, then," she said. "What category?"

"Suicides," said Wacko.

"It stands to reason," said Buzz. "They just want out. So why should *they* ever come back as ghosts?"

"Whatever the reason," said Wacko, "that is the fact."

"So don't any of you go killing yourselves, thinking you can come back and enjoy seeing people grieving over you," said Buzz. "Because you won't!"

"I'll bear it in mind," sighed the vanquished Tessa.

"A very good point, Robert," said Mr. Holly. "That is—um—it would be if there were such things as ghosts. Which—um—of course there *might* be. You've both made out a very good case."

"Maybe some of the audience would like to ask questions," said Miss Perrins, kindly sparing Tessa and Dwayne, who were finally speechless.

There was a scuffling sound.

"Yes, please!"

One of the youngest kids, a girl on the front row, had stood up.

"Yes?" said Miss Perrins.

"I'd like to know if—if there isn't *any* way a ghost can make—can sort of make a living person know he's there? Or she?"

"Well—"

"Well—"

Both Buzz and Wacko started to answer at the same time. They grinned at each other and bowed slightly— after you.

"Don't answer, don't answer! Don't either of you answer!" Carlos was almost beside himself with impatience by now. "Look at the time, you fools!"

"Yeah—time, I think, that we ought to let them know we're here," said Joe. "Carlos, you give Wacko the red alert signal. Danny, you take Buzz."

Buzz was already speaking.

"Let me make this clear," he was saying. "Ghosts can make themselves felt by each other. They can see and hear and touch each other, just like they were still alive. But no matter how hard a ghost hits a living person, the blow—"

He gave a start, and paused. Danny had just pressed firmly on Buzz's upper lip, below the nose.

"—it—uh—feels like a very faint flick, like a fly might just have brushed the spot."

"Yes," said Wacko, thoughtfully rubbing *his* lip, where Carlos had just jabbed it. "And not everyone is sensitive enough to feel it."

"Unless, of course, they know to expect it," said Buzz, giving Wacko a questioning look.

"Baloney!" said someone in the audience—a fat kid called Chester Adams, whom Buzz and Wacko had had trouble with before.

"Order!" said Mr. Holly.

"OK!" said Carlos, forgetting his impatience as he stared at his old enemy and grinned. "You've asked for this, Chester!"

"Carlos! Come back here!" cried Joe, seeing his colleague dart off, down the platform steps, straight for Chester, who was sitting at the end of a row.

Mr. Holly was just asking if there were any more questions and a whole forest of arms had shot up, when Carlos hit Chester on the nose. Not just once or twice, but a whole battery of punches.

"Ah-a-*choo!*" sneezed Chester, rubbing his nose.

"What's the trouble, Chester?" said the girl next to him. "Did a ghost touch *you?*"

She was laughing, but the laugh slipped some when she felt a faint flick-flick on her right earlobe.

"Oh! Oh, *no!*" she yelped. "I think *I* just felt something!"

And in the next couple of minutes, kids all over the auditorium were laughing or yelling—some with fear, some with delight, most with a mixture of the two.

As Joe and the other ghosts could plainly see, Carlos was responsible for only three or four of these. The rest were simply imagining they'd been touched. But it looked like it would turn into pandemonium before very long.

"Why—it's mass hysteria!" gasped Miss Perrins.

"Leave it to me!" growled Mr. Holly.

Then he grabbed the microphone, turned the volume up a couple of decibels and said:

"All right, all right! Order! Order! Stop fooling around, and we'll take the vote. All those in favor of the motion—that This House Does Not Believe in Ghosts—raise their right hands."

The practical command—plus a genuine concern to register their opinions—had an immediate calming effect on the audience.

A mere 23 hands were raised, sharply contrasting with the 184 against the motion, a few minutes later.

"And those 184 included some of our firmest supporters," said Tessa, sadly. But she was a good kid and she very quickly held out her hand, first to Wacko, then Buzz. "Hey! Congratulations! You did a beautiful job. And all out of thin air, too!"

There was a stirring in the "thin air" behind the two victors.

"Now maybe we can get on with the real work," said Carlos, reaching out to give Wacko's upper lip another reminder.

But his finger never made it. He felt his wrist being grabbed, and a voice that didn't belong to any of the other three rasped, "Just a second, *you!*"

Carlos stared up at the newcomer, who continued to hold his wrist in a cruel, sharply painful grip. The others stared, too. They'd been so busy following the progress of the debate and watching its effect on the living members of the audience that they hadn't realized there'd been one more ghost present, lurking somewhere in the shadows at the back of the platform.

Karen gasped.

"Why! It's *Roscoe!*"

The grip on Carlos's wrist tightened so hard that he yelled out. Then the newcomer flung Carlos's hand free and swiftly turned toward Karen. His face was suddenly creased with alert malevolent curiosity.

"How do *you* know my name, girlie?" he said, in a slow menacing snarl.

4
Roscoe

As the meeting broke up and the kids began to file out, still talking about the debate, a tense, curious interview took place on the platform.

"Well—because—because—" stammered Karen, shrinking back as she tried to answer the stranger's question.

"Because it was in the local papers," said Joe, stepping between the two and tensing his shoulders. "You were the guy shot in that burglary at the Hymans' place, weren't you? The jewelry store on Railroad Street?"

The other had pulled himself up sharply. He was about nineteen, lean and lithe as a cat, with short blond hair and hard blue eyes. He looked tough and very, very mean. But compared to Joe, he was slightly built, and just then Joe himself was looking very tough and mean.

"Yeah!" the newcomer growled. "I was shot all right. Right here!"

He patted his chest, near the left shoulder. He was wearing a dark blue long-sleeved shirt and black jeans. They were the clothes he'd been wearing on the night of the burglary, but there was no sign of a bullet hole in the shirt, or of the slashes made by the emergency-room nurses when they cut it off his back, or even of any blood.

The other ghosts weren't surprised. They knew that when anyone came back as a ghost, they usually wore the clothes they felt best in, or most comfortable in, around the date of their death. And no matter how dreadful an accident they'd met with, neither their clothes nor their bodies ever showed any of the mess or damage.

After all, Karen herself had been run over by a truck, Danny had been buried under tons of bricks and Joe had fallen from the tenth floor of a building. Only Carlos had had a less messy death than Roscoe, having been electrocuted during one of his experiments.

"So—uh—you didn't pull through?" Carlos said now, trying to make it sound as if he didn't know *too* much. "You died of the wound?"

"Yeah—worse luck!" snarled Roscoe. "Or, believe me, the copper who did this to me, *he'd* be the one mooching around as a ghost, not me!"

He meant it, too. The others knew this. Roscoe was just the type to haul himself out of a hospital bed, oozing blood through the bandages, and go in search of revenge. Even if it killed him.

"How long have you been back?" said Joe, trying

to sound merely casually interested, one ghost to another.

He darted a sharp glance at Carlos and the other two, hoping they'd have the sense to leave the talking to him.

Roscoe shrugged.

"Four, five days. But what happened between me croaking and coming back like this beats me. All those weeks. Just a lousy blank."

"It usually does take three or four months," said Joe. "In most cases, anyway."

"So they tell me," muttered Roscoe. "Waste of time, in my opinion. And it lets the trail go cold."

Carlos couldn't help interrupting here. The comment about the trail going cold had set him thinking hard and fast. He was wondering if Roscoe had somehow gotten wind that the four ghosts he was talking to had actually been present at the shooting— had even been responsible for alerting the police to the attempted burglary.

"Was—was there something special you wanted me for just now?" he said.

Roscoe turned, but without showing any special signs of hostility.

"Yeah. I was listening to those two guys talking about ghosts. They seemed to know *something* about what it's like, and I was wondering if I could pick up a few pointers. Then I see you touching those kids down there and at least getting them to feel you. Especially that fat creep."

"Chester?" said Carlos. "Chester Adams?"

"That his name? The one who sneezed? Yeah. He's

why I was here in the first place. I've been following him around. He's my only lead in all this."

"In all what?" asked Joe, with another warning look at Carlos.

"In finding out who snitched on me and my buddy that night. Because whoever it was . . ."

He didn't finish. He didn't have to. His eyes were blazing like a panther's when it's just about to pounce. He was clutching and unclutching his fists, making his fingers seem more like long whitish yellow claws. Karen suppressed a shudder. First Vinnie, now this, she was thinking. The living and the dead, and both of them monsters. Oh, boy! This looks like it's going to be *some* Halloween!

"Why Chester?" Joe asked calmly.

Roscoe shrugged.

"Oh, I don't know! Just a hunch, I guess. I do remember me and my buddy having a meal at the kid's father's place. That greasy spoon joint a few doors away from the Hymans. That's when we were casing the jewelry store. Maybe he overheard something he shouldn't have."

The others knew all about that occasion, too. They knew that the only ones who'd overheard anything in the Adams's diner that evening had been Joe and Danny. But they knew better than to say so. After all, Chester was in no immediate danger. They, on the other hand, would be, if Roscoe ever suspected the truth. In very grave danger indeed.

Carlos rubbed his wrist.

"So what did you want me for?" he said.

"To ask you if there's no way of getting the fat jerk

to know there's a ghost who'd like a word with him. Maybe scare the truth outa him. Is there?"

Joe shook his head.

"No. No way. The best you could ever do is what you've seen Carlos, here, do already. Make him feel like there are flies around. But after a while, when nothing else happens, he'll just shrug it off and think he's got some minor skin condition."

Roscoe looked dejected, but still vicious.

"Yeah! Too bad *he* isn't a ghost. *Then* he'd hear me. Then I could really get to work on him. Then I could choke it out of him, *rip* it out of him! . . . Anyways, I'll keep following him. Maybe he'll drop something to one of his buddies. And maybe I *will* find a way of getting through, at that." He fell silent, his jaws working steadily. He seemed to be grinding his teeth. Then he shrugged, and loped away down the platform steps. "See y'around!" he muttered, without glancing back.

"Whew!" Danny watched him leave the auditorium. "Roscoe back! As a Malev!"

This was the word used by ghosts for the hating ones—the word Buzz had nearly blurted out during the debate.

"Yeah!" murmured Joe, looking worried. "Let's hope he doesn't fall in with some of the older Malevs and learn some of *their* tricks!"

"Let's hope he doesn't find out about the part *we* played," said Karen.

"Or about the other two," said Danny. "And the part *they* played."

"You're right," said Joe. "Which is why it's doubly important now to talk to Buzz and Wacko. Come on!"

5
The Haunted Word Processor

Wacko's room was long and low, at the top of the house. At one end, there was a bed, half-concealed in a recess, with a chest of drawers, a clothes closet and other bedroom stuff. At the other end, it was more like a laboratory workshop. There was a huge rectangular table that stretched almost the full width of the room, in front of the window. It was littered with tools and instruments and charts, with tiny electronics components scattered around at one end.

But in the center of the table there was a clear space. And in that space was a large gray word processor. The machine didn't have a brand name stamped or stenciled on it. The casing itself looked pretty rough, as if whatever care had gone into the design must have been lavished on its interior working parts.

Which it had.

Wacko and Carlos (when he'd been alive) had built

that word processor themselves. Carlos had been the brains behind it. At the age of thirteen, he was already acknowledged as an electronics genius, the marvel of his parents and even his teachers. Wacko was also good at electronics—the best in the school, if not the whole town, *now*—but he'd always been way behind his friend.

One thing special about the word processor was that they'd designed it for operation on micro-micro-currents. Another thing—even more special—was something they didn't find out until several months after Carlos's death. . . .

The machine was switched on just after 4:30 that afternoon. The daylight was beginning to fade, making the screen's green glow seem all the brighter. It was reflected on the expectant faces of Buzz and Wacko whenever they glanced at it—which was often. They were sitting at the table, but slightly sideways and about three feet apart, leaving a space directly in front of the machine itself.

After still another glance at the screen, then at his watch, Buzz said: "You're sure *you* felt the red alert signal, too?"

"Positive," said Wacko, fingering his lip again.

"Do you think we stood long enough at the door downstairs, leaving it open for them?"

"Sure! I could have sworn they were with us when we came in."

"And the second time, when you went down to make sure?"

"Positive," said Wacko again. "Though I still think

34

they came through the first time. My guess is they're playing some kind of trick. . . . Hey, come on, you guys!" he said to the room behind them.

Buzz was shaking his head.

"Not if it was really a red alert," he said. "They wouldn't fool around then."

"So maybe it's such a complicated matter it's taking time to sort out everything they have to report. They— *ah!*"

Wacko broke off. The screen had begun to flicker.

> *"You bet it's complicated! You're absolutely right, Wacko! Hi, Buzz! Sorry, you guys, for keeping you waiting. But the full Ghost Squad is now in session. . . ."*

Neither boy had touched the keyboard. Nobody and nothing had, in fact. The activation had been brought about by Carlos, standing in that space between them, bending over the machine, swaying, and stabbing the air above the keys with his fingers, only millimeters away, but without touching them.

Touching them would have been useless for a ghost. Two of the other three, who were watching intently, even suspected that the swaying and stabbing was useless too—that it was all part of Carlos's love of drama, his tendency to make a circus act out of even the most ordinary processes.

35

But Joe Armstrong didn't think so. He had a feeling that Carlos really needed to go through those motions to help him concentrate so fiercely and accurately the jets and streams of micro-micro-energy that would set in motion the machine's delicate processes.

Through the screen, Carlos continued:

*"First we have to tell you—*dummies!*—that you went too far this afternoon in that debate. You were giving away much too much, and you could have given some people ideas—ideas that could have blown the whole operation. . . ."*

As they received their dressing-down, Buzz and Wacko cast uneasy glances behind them. There was no need to see the other four. They could imagine only too well the frowns of disapproval on their faces—especially Joe's, as he reminded Carlos what to transmit.

For if Carlos was the scientific genius who had made the stupendous breakthrough possible, it was Joe who had organized them into a group that could put that breakthrough to good use.

"I mean, OK," he had said, right at the start. "It may not help us in our own personal missions. We can't send Buzz and Wacko with messages to our loved ones, telling them not to worry, that we're still around as ghosts, and doing fine, and making contact through a fancy typewriter. I mean, who'd believe them?"

"Not my mom, not even my kid brothers and sisters," Danny had said glumly, thinking of how much his family had depended on him for material things, not just words of cheer.

"Not my father," said Karen, "even though he is making himself sick, thinking—wrongly—that he was to blame for my death."

"My folks would just get mad, thinking Buzz and Wacko were playing nasty tricks," said Carlos. "They'd get so mad that *I* wouldn't like to be in Buzz and Wacko's shoes, no, sir! No way!"

"And my wife would think they were crazy and report them to the police," said Joe. "But—hey!—never mind. There is one way we could be doing some good."

And then he'd gone on to talk about the crimes that they and all ghosts can see going on all around them every day—sometimes with the criminals getting away with it, other times with innocent people taking the blame.

"Through Buzz and Wacko," he had said finally, "we can give warnings to possible victims, alert the cops to the real perpetrators, maybe even prevent crimes."

And that was how the Ghost Squad had come into being. In the five months they had been active, it hadn't been anywhere near as easy as it had sounded at first. But they had prevented a jewel heist—the one in which Roscoe had taken part—and probably saved at least two innocent lives at the same time. And they had helped to bring a couple of murderers to book, even though the four ghosts had had to go all the way to London, hitching a ride on Concorde to do it.

That had been back in July. Since then, they'd had no major crime to tackle. But they hadn't been idle. Instead, they'd made use of the time and their special ghost advantages by helping to find missing articles and pets, and pointing Buzz and Wacko to their whereabouts. So the two boys were able to restore quite a number of these missing articles or creatures to their owners and collect any rewards that had been offered. That way, they hoped to be able to build up a fund that could be used for expenses when tackling future crimes. Doing the legwork for the Ghost Squad didn't always come cheap.

"But nobody *really* believed us!" said Wacko, answering the others' complaint about the debate. "We didn't give away all *that* much, surely?"

"They just thought we were making it up," said Buzz. "Miss Perrins told me so, after the debate."

"*Sure!*" flickered the reply. "*That's what Miss Perrins thought and Mr. Holly thought, and no doubt all the kids listening thought, all the living listeners. But how about if other ghosts had been present?* They'd *realize you were telling the truth, the real facts, wouldn't they? And that would get them thinking: How come these two kids know so much? Have they been able to make contact?*"

Buzz and Wacko looked at each other. Wacko was beginning to sweat. Buzz gulped.

"Yeah—but—but there were only *you* guys there. Uh—weren't there?"

"And you'd have given us the warning signal, wouldn't you?" said Wacko, wiping his forehead and brightening up. "You'd have touched us under our chins, wouldn't you?"

"*Sure! But supposing we hadn't noticed any other ghosts present? Suppose we were so busy admiring your beautiful, big-deal, world-class debating techniques? You jerks!*"

Carlos was getting steamed up. He suddenly collected himself. He turned to Joe doubtfully.

Joe smiled grimly and nodded.

"Go on, Carlos. You're doing fine. Tell 'em. Hit 'em with Roscoe!"

Carlos turned back to the keyboard.

"And in fact there was one present, one other ghost besides us. Luckily, he was a rookie ghost, just arrived."

Wacko chewed his lower lip. Buzz sighed.

"Oh, well, that's OK then," he murmured.

"But he was a Malev, you dumbbells! And—are you ready for this?—his name is Roscoe!*"*

The two boys started. The sweat broke out again on Wacko's forehead.

"R-Roscoe?"

"Yes. Roscoe."

"The—*the* Roscoe? The one that—?"

"Yes! That Roscoe! All burning up and raring for revenge on whoever blew the whistle on him. What else could he *be but a Malev?"*

Then Carlos, through the screen, with promptings from Joe and the others, told a deathly silent Buzz and Wacko of the encounter on the school platform. After which—and before the two debaters could feel any relief from the fact that so far Roscoe hadn't a clue about whom he was seeking—Joe, through Carlos, started in giving them a rundown of what would happen if any of the older, more experienced Malevs got wind of their breakthrough.

"To make contact with living people, to be able to operate directly through living people, is just what every Malev dreams of," the warning continued. *"They'd give anything for the secret. They'd stop at nothing. Our lives—correction: our* after*lives—wouldn't be worth a cent!"*

"Gosh!" murmured Buzz. "I—I just didn't think . . ."

"We—we're awfully sorry!" said Wacko. "Honestly! We didn't mean to put you in any danger!"

"*Us? Us in danger? It isn't only us, you dope! You'd be in danger, too. Terrible danger!*"

The two boys frowned.

"Yeah—well—but not in *physical* danger, the way you guys would be," said Wacko.

"I mean, I know I tried to throw a scare into the kids during the debate by suggesting the *possibility*," said Buzz. "But like you told Roscoe, there's not really any way a ghost could hurt *us* physically. Uh—is there?"

"*That's only what we told Roscoe to keep him quiet for a while. But of course there are ways a really experienced Malev can harm a living person if he sets his mind to it! Did you want us to draw Roscoe a picture?*"

"But—but how?"

Carlos turned to Joe.

"Hey—I don't know about Buzz—but Wacko can get very, very nervous!"

"Doesn't matter," said the leader of the Ghost Squad. "They need to know. They have to know. It's time they knew. Draw *them* the picture."

6
Danger:
Malevs at Work!

"Let's just start in a small way," Carlos began. *"You already know about some of the things any ghost can do to affect the living world. By exerting the micro-micro-micro-energy we've all got—exerting it on objects that are in a very delicate state of balance, very hair-trigger, very, very light. Like me, right now, with these word-processor circuits."*

"Sure!" said Wacko, blinking at the screen. "And like Joe, when he gives something that's ju-u-u-st ready to drop off a shelf that tiny extra tilt and—crash!"

"Or that other thing you were telling us about once," said Buzz. "Where you use the energy to attract minute particles of moisture in a mist. Getting it to cluster around your arms or heads or bodies. Creating ghostly shapes that even living people can see."

"Or the swarm of gnats that Karen got to cluster around her that time," said Wacko. "But what does this have to do with Roscoe physically harming us?"

Buzz grinned.

"Do you think he might try to have us gnat-bitten to death?"

"SHUT UP!!"

The screen seemed to yell the two words.

Then the message continued in a more normal, less furious, almost an icily calm form.

"Things like that take a whole lot of effort and a whole lot of practice, but they can be done by most ghosts. So Malevs—and here's where we start wiping those stupid grins off your faces—can do the same things. Even better, with all their fierce energy. Only they don't bother to make fancy shapes or just play pranks. Oh, no!"

Then Carlos and the others, through the screen, went on to tell the two watching boys—with the green reflection on their faces getting stronger in the gathering dusk—of some of the uses various Malevs had been able to make of this peculiar skill.

Like:

The Malev who had managed to gather together a small dense strip of mist, no longer and no wider than his forearm, and hold it against the windshield of a living enemy's car so that it obscured his view when cornering at a high speed. . . .

The Malev who once diverted a flock of bees across three fields, to where an old enemy—a landscape painter—was working at his easel. That enemy—as the Malev well knew—was allergic to bee stings. And the Malev made sure the swarm completely enveloped the painter. . . .

The Malev—a female this time—who choked her hated ex-husband to death with a feather. She worked so hard and so strenuously on a single, small, fluffy, pigeon feather, airborne on a light summer breeze, that she got it to drift to the hammock where the man was snoozing. His constant snoring had bugged her terribly during her life with him, but this time she was counting on it. And indeed he was snoring now. And into his open snoring mouth, she steered that feather, and down over the lolling tongue, and straight into the vital aperture that led to his air passage.

A Chance in a Million! the papers said.

Which it was.

The lady Malev could so easily have failed.

But she didn't. . . .

The two boys began to stir restlessly.

"Sure, sure!" said Wacko, before Carlos could go on. "That's very impressive. But Roscoe would never catch *us* like that, even if he was out to get us. *He* wouldn't be skillful enough."

"And I don't snore," said Buzz, laughing. "How about you, Wacko?"

"*Hey! Hold it!*" said the screen. "*Don't go laughing your dumb heads off yet! The picture's only just beginning to take shape. There is something that even the rawest Malev can do—once the possibility is pointed out. It means certain extinction for the Malev, but not before he's had the satisfaction of killing his living enemy—or seeing him killed.*"

Wacko licked his lips.

"Huh—how?"

"Possession."

"What?"

"You can read, Buzz. Po-ssess-ion. Where a Malev steps right inside a living body and takes possession of it."

"You're not saying—?"

"We're saying it's done all the time. You've heard the saying, 'So-and-so is stoned out of his mind.' Or: 'So-and-so is out of his skull.' Or: 'So-and-so's mind is wandering.' Or: 'So-and-so didn't hear a word because he was miles away— you could tell by his eyes.' Or even, 'Bless you!'—when someone sneezes—because the sneeze has temporarily blown his soul out of his body and something evil might step in and takes its place if the sneezer isn't blessed quick."

"What's this got to do with Malevs?"

"Because Malevs—any ghosts, but Malevs are usually the ones who do it—they can move in on a living person's body. When that person is very drunk. Or drugged. Or hypnotized. Or spaced-out in any other way."

"So what use is that?" said Buzz. "To a Malev?"

"What use?! Why, if that living person is an enemy, then the Malev can drive him to do anything, once the Malev's taken possession. Like jump over a cliff. Or out of a high window. Or kill himself some other way. Like I said, the Malev usually self-destructs, too, just with the tremendous effort. He burns out. But what does he care? He's achieved his aim, hasn't he?"

"Wow!" murmured Wacko. "Like a kamikaze pilot!"

"Exactly!"

"But *we* don't drink, or anything like that," said Buzz, looking serious now.

"No, but you could get sick and delirious. That would give a Malev his opportunity, if you were an enemy. But it

44

doesn't have to be your *body he uses. He could use the body of some nearby drunk, or junky, or crazy person, and have him kill you. Just sort of go berserk—yeah. That's what it would look like. But with the knife or gun or whatever especially directed at* you!"

There was a blank on the screen for a few moments. Wacko took the opportunity to switch on the overhead light. He guessed that Carlos would be consulting with one of the others.

He was right. Danny was reminding Carlos of something else. Then:

"*Oh, yeah!*" came the message. "*And one other thing. This really did happen to you, Buzz. The time that Danny managed to wake you. Remember?*"

Buzz had started. Then he nodded.

"Yes. Yes, you told me at the time. Danny couldn't possibly have roused me directly, by yelling or touching. But I was having one of those dreams where I was watching myself sleeping, and—"

"*Right! Your own built-in ghost—your astral body, the same as everyone's got, only most people don't realize it— your built-in ghost stepped out of your body for a few moments. And Danny was able to get his message through to that—ghost to ghost.*"

Buzz was frowning.

"Yes, but how would that help Roscoe? All he could do would be to wake me up."

"*Oh, yeah? How about putting you to sleep? For keeps? By clobbering your astral body—and Roscoe could do it with his bare hands, so long as he's using them on another ghost— and then stepping inside you in its place. Then—well—I already told you what might happen then.*"

45

Buzz and Wacko were very silent now. They didn't need any other argument.

"You've—uh—drawn us the picture, Carlos," said Buzz, after a while. "And we certainly get it. Right, Wacko?"

"Sh—" Wacko wanted to say, "Sure do!"—but the words stuck in his throat, like the feather in the Malev's ex-husband's throat.

He nodded jerkily instead.

"So be careful!" warned the screen. *"Watch your tongues. Don't ever mention the jewelry heist or Roscoe, not even between yourselves. Especially your part in it, and how you warned Detective Grogan. You never know when Roscoe might be around, now he's a ghost. And once he hears anything like that—bingo!"*

Wacko swallowed hard.

"Yeah. Sure. Are you—are you certain—?"

His eyes were flitting to every corner of the room.

"Oh, that's OK," said the screen. *"He's nowhere near now. He isn't gonna catch us napping twice. From now on, we're keeping our eyes peeled for Roscoe at all times. . . . Anyway, now for the main business of the meeting. We've stumbled into a pretty gruesome case."*

The two helpers sighed gently.

They were both thinking the same thing.

However gruesome the case might be, it couldn't be one half as grisly as what they'd just heard.

Which is where they were mistaken again.

Very much mistaken.

7
"A-haunting We Will Go!"

There was one thing they were soon all very sure about, however: The Halloween Conspiracy presented them with some extremely tricky problems.

"It *ought* to be simple," said Wacko thoughtfully, after Carlos had given his report about what they'd seen and heard at the Boyars residence. "Just a matter of calling the police and telling *them* about it."

"Yeah," said Buzz. "But then what? What would we tell them when they asked us how we knew so much about Vinnie's plans?"

"And since he's one of the senator's immediate family, the cops would be even less likely to believe it," said Wacko. "I mean, Vinnie doesn't have any police record, as far as I know. How about you guys? Do you know of any?"

There was a pause. Then:

"No. Vinnie's just a private, sneaky Nasty. And you're right. The cops would have to have some really solid evidence before they acted on a tip-off like that."

Buzz was chewing his lip. He looked at Wacko.

"How about warning the housekeeper—What'ser-name—young Lester's grandmother?"

"Josephine?" said Wacko. He smiled ruefully. "No. . . . She'd never believe it, either. Even though she probably knows how nasty Vinnie can get. She's a kind of gentle, religious woman who likes to believe the best about everybody."

"Yeah! Until it's too late. I know the type," said Buzz. "Poor stiffs!"

Wacko shrugged.

"Anyway, that's the way she'd react. And besides, even if she did believe it and she went and told the senator—the blame would still backfire on Lester. Vinnie would make sure of *that*. He's halfway there to framing the kid already, isn't he? He'd just say that Josephine was trying to cover for Lester."

"And would the senator believe him? Knowing Vinnie?"

"Why not? The senator knows young Lester, too, remember. And even though Lester doesn't have any nastiness in him, well—he is kind of—uh—strange. You know—not really capable of judging the probable results of his actions."

"But Lester wouldn't—"

"Oh, *I* know that, and *you* know that! But it would be easier for the senator to believe that someone like Lester would try such a thing, not really knowing what he was doing, than that his stepson Vinnie would *risk* such a thing. Because whatever Vinnie is, he isn't dumb."

"That's true," murmured Buzz. "Just vicious. Vicious Vinnie."

The ghosts had been listening intently.

"Ask them," said Joe, "what are the chances of warning Lester himself?"

Carlos grinned. He didn't even bother to turn to the keyboard.

"Forget it, Joe! I know Lester, too. He's a nice kid, like Wacko says, but really slow, and kinda innocent. He'd just blow everything by going up to Vinnie and saying, nice and quiet and politely, 'Excuse me, sir. *Why* did you put needles in the candy?' Something dumb like that. Then I wouldn't give much for Lester's hide."

"Carlos is right, Joe," said Danny. "Let's leave Lester out of this."

Joe nodded, frowning.

"But we have to stop them, that's for sure. We can't let the trick-or-treaters eat those chocolate bars, or even get near them. Tell Buzz and Wacko *that*."

This time, Carlos carried out the order.

Buzz and Wacko got the point.

"Maybe if one of *us* told the senator, he'd listen," said Buzz. "If we gave him the full details. After all, he must have *some* idea of what Vinnie's capable of. At least he'd give it serious attention—possibly break open a bar or two to see if there *are* any needles."

"Yes," Wacko agreed. "And that's what it might come down to. But that brings us to another problem." He turned. "Didn't you guys say you heard

Vinnie mention something about the senator's schedule? That he wouldn't be returning from Belgium until Saturday afternoon, just before the party? That doesn't leave us much time to contact him."

Karen turned to Joe.

"He's right, there," she said. "And getting to see a public figure like the senator, when he's only just arrived and busy with reporters and last-minute arrangements—well—it won't be very easy."

Danny swallowed. He'd been thinking about those kids and the chocolate bars and the way *he'd* enjoyed chocolate bars, whenever he could afford them. It wouldn't be like eating fish or something, where you know there might be bones. You just stuck the old bar in, and bit, and champed on it. Sort of hearty . . .

"It would mean waiting until the last minute, too," he said. "And can we *risk* that?"

Carlos was wincing. The same chocolate-champing picture had been flashing through his mind.

"Maybe there's something else we could be doing," he said. "Maybe—hey! yeah!—maybe we could warn Vinnie off. Get Buzz and Wacko to phone him and let him know he's been under observation."

Joe shook his head.

"Huh-*uh!* That might trigger an even bigger crime."

"Like what?" said Karen.

"Murder. I mean, you saw and heard this guy. He's half-crazy. And if he gets a call proving some outsiders know all the details of his plot, he'll go even crazier."

"So?"

"So he'll think there's only one person in the world

50

who could have blabbered those details to the callers."

Karen's eyes had widened.

"Oh . . . yes. . . . The woman. Jeanine. And you think he might—"

"Kill her? Yes. He'd probably think she'd been setting him up for some kind of blackmail squeeze. *Sure* he might kill her. He'd be mad and he'd be scared, and with a psycho like him, that could easily be enough."

"She's rotten herself, anyway," said Carlos. "I mean, better risk *her* life than any of those kids' lives."

"Sure. But rotten though she is, we don't want her death on our consciences, do we?"

Karen, Carlos and Danny shook their heads.

"Hey, you guys! You still there?"

Buzz's cry reminded them that voices didn't travel both ways between ghosts and the living.

"*Sorry!*" said Carlos, over the screen.

Then he explained the problem about the woman.

Neither Buzz nor Wacko could see any way around it.

"OK," said Joe. "So let's leave it for the moment. Because there is one thing they can be doing. Get them to call the senator's office in the state capitol and find out exactly what his movements will be on Saturday."

"Will do!" said Wacko, when the message had been translated.

He spoke confidently. His father worked in the capitol, in the state's attorney's office. Wacko knew he could count on Mr. Williams's help in obtaining this information, even if he and Buzz couldn't get it direct.

"But isn't there anything *you* guys could be doing?" said Buzz. "I mean like trying to spook Vinnie or the woman? Rattle their nerves? Get them to feel they're being haunted and had better watch their step? Huh? . . . Like using some of those Malev techniques, but in a good cause. And," he added, grinning a little, "without, of course, going in for any kamikaze attacks!"

It went down better than he'd imagined.

"Hey! Wow! Yeah!" cried Carlos. "We could try!"

"It's an idea!" said Danny, almost as eagerly.

Even Joe seemed to brighten at the thought.

"Maybe," he drawled, thinking hard. "Maybe we could cause a few things to fall off shelves. Stuff like that." He frowned. "The only sure way, though, would be if either Vinnie or Jeanine had one of those special dreams, with their astral bodies taking a little space walk. Then we could warn them off face-to-face. They'd think it was a dream, maybe—but they wouldn't dare ignore it."

"Sure, sure!" said Carlos. "Or if they got drunk or something. Vinnie might."

Joe made up his mind.

"It's worth trying, anyway," he said. "Danny—you can join me. We'll go visit Vinnie again. Spend the night there, if necessary. . . . Karen and Carlos, you two find out where Jeanine lives and—"

"I already know where she lives," said Karen. "At least, I know the apartment building, near where I— uh—*used* to live. I've seen her going in and out there lots of times."

"Terrific!" said Joe. "So you and Carlos can take care of her. Meanwhile, Carlos, thank Buzz for his suggestion. Tell him we'll be getting onto it right away. And tell them both we'll meet them here straight after school tomorrow, and compare notes."

The other three could hardly wait.

"Hurry it up, Carlos!" said Karen, already moving to the door. "Tell Wacko to look sharp and let us out. Then . . ."

"Then *what?*" said Danny, when she broke off and started to laugh in a queer gurgling undertone.

"Oh, sorry, Danny!" she said, her eyes sparkling. "I didn't mean to scare *you*. I was just practicing my old Halloween witch-laugh. . . . I was going to say, 'Then a-haunting we will go!' "

8
"The Devil's Pasteboards!"

Even as early as 6:30 in the evening, the residence of Senator Boyars had a spooky look. There was a cover of thin high cloud overhead that diffused the light from the nearly full moon in a powdery blue white dusting, picking out the portico and the pillars at the front of the house—a sparkling white during the day—and giving them a faint, sinister glow that made the structure look more like a gigantic mausoleum than a dwelling place for the living.

Strengthening this impression was the fact that the house was in darkness, except for a dim, reddish-colored lantern over the main door and a greenish light in a window on the first floor, in a corner room to the left of the portico. It was like the tomb of some great and terrible prince, set on its hill, with the lamp to warn off any inquisitive strangers and the green-lit window to remind would-be intruders that the place had a custodian—a custodian with a macabre taste in illuminations and probably weird unearthly powers.

"It's a perfect setting for Saturday's Halloween bash," said Joe, as they walked up the driveway. "I'll say that!"

"Yeah," grunted Danny. "Except it'll probably be all lit up then. I used to deliver the evening papers here, and when the senator's home, it's like a hotel. Lights all over the place."

He cast a glance back—beyond the blue black mass of the trees by the main gate, and gazed wistfully at the orange glow beyond them, where the town lay.

"I never did like it here when the senator wasn't home," he murmured. "Too spooky."

Joe laughed and clapped him on the shoulder.

"It shouldn't scare you *now*," he said. "Anyway, our problem tonight is will Vinnie be home. And how to get in and join him if he is."

They had reached the steps leading up to the stone terrace in front of the building, behind the pillars. The door looked very solid in the lantern's glow. And now that they were close enough, they could see a smaller yellowish white spot of light, shining from a button at the side of the door.

"There's the bell," said Danny. "Maybe we should—" Then he broke off, smiling foolishly. "Sorry! I forgot. I was still thinking about being one nervous newsboy."

"Maybe we should give it a ring?" said Joe. He was stooping, peering at it. "That isn't so dumb as you may think, Danny. Given a loose connection, an experienced ghost can do wonders with bells." He straightened up and sighed. "But not with this one. Seems in pretty good shape to me."

"Let's see if we can see anything at the lighted window," said Danny. "Maybe it's just one of those automatic antiburglar lamps. Maybe there's nobody home at all, yet."

At first, as they approached the corner of the building, it looked as if they might be in for another disappointment. The greenish light, they now discovered, was caused by the color of the drapes—and the drapes were drawn.

"I sure hope Carlos and Karen are having better luck," said Danny. "Because, if you ask me—"

"You're too much of a pessimist, Danny!" There was a lilt of triumph in Joe's voice as he turned from the chink he'd found, where the drapes didn't quite meet. "Come take a look."

Danny bent to the crack. Then he grinned.

"Vinnie!" he said. "He is home, after all." He frowned. "But what's he doing *this* time?"

Judging from the bookshelves in the background, Vinnie was in some kind of a library. But he wasn't reading.

He was sitting at a table, but facing away from it. He had something in his left hand, obscured by the top of the table, and he kept plucking something from it with his other hand. Plucking and flicking—and the flicking was so fast that it was just a blur at first, and there was no chance of seeing the objects as they fell because that part of the room was out of the ghosts' range of vision.

56

Then suddenly Joe laughed.

"It's cards!" he said. "Playing cards. He's flipping cards into a hat or something. Vinnie's just passing time, Danny. It's as innocent as that."

"Huh!" Danny grunted as he strained to get a better focus. "He doesn't seem to be enjoying it much, anyway. He's still got that mean look."

Danny was right. That was why it had taken him so long to realize that this was just a trivial game. Vinnie's face was set in impatient, bitter lines. The dimpled chin jutted angrily. The eyes were hard and glittering. Even the tight smile did nothing to relieve that expression. It was all too obviously a sneer—aimed at someone or something in his thoughts.

Danny remembered hearing somewhere that playing cards were often called the Devil's pasteboards. Now he could believe it.

"Maybe he's expecting someone and they're late," said Joe. "Maybe he's waiting for Jeanine."

"Yeah. Maybe Carlos and Karen will be joining us, after all."

When Vinnie got up, empty-handed, and went out of sight to retrieve the cards, Joe said, "We'd better be ready for whenever someone does arrive. It'll be the only way we'll get into this house tonight."

"Maybe there's an open window someplace," said Danny.

"One without a screen? And open wide *enough?* Fat chance!"

Danny smiled.

"Hey! Who's the pessimist now? At least we can take a look, can't we?"

But of course Joe was right. And they were just approaching the green-draped window again, when the headlights of a car swept across the front of the building and they saw the vehicle's small hunched shape come chugging up the driveway.

"It isn't the senator in his Fleetwood, that's for sure!" said Danny, grinning, as the old VW came lurching past them and up along the side of the house.

"It isn't Jeanine, either," said Joe.

The car had stopped, and a small elderly lady was getting out, sighing heavily.

"No. It's Josephine," said Danny. "And that's Lester, still messing around unfastening his seat belt."

The two ghosts moved in close as Lester finally made it with the buckle and Josephine headed for a side door of the house.

"I done it, Gramma!" said the boy.

Lester was twelve and big for his age. He was rather flabby without being fat. Even in the moonglow, they could see he was dressed very smartly in a grown-up style—with a shirt and tie and a neat sport jacket.

But he wasn't nearly so grown-up in his speech and his movements. These were rather slow and hesitant—the movements of someone who seemed to find it hard to walk and talk at the same time—a fact that was welcomed by the ghosts, because the woman was a quick mover, once she was out of her car.

"Come *on*, Lester!" she said, gently but impatiently, as she stood by the door, key in hand. "Don't you go talking all night. I got work to do, and we're late already."

"Yeah, Gramma. Sure. But you didn't answer me,

Gramma. *Why* did the little guy shoot the big guy?"

"Because he was bad. Now come on, or I won't take you to the movies no more."

Josephine turned the key in the lock.

"Yeah, but—"

"Come *on*, Lester!"

"—but *who* was bad? The big guy or—?"

"The big one. OK? So come on in, now. And hurry up and close the door. You're letting the cold air in. And the senator, he'll have to pay for the extra heating."

This argument obviously counted with Lester. Quickly, for him, he stepped inside and closed the door. But the ghosts were way ahead of him, following Josephine as she switched on the lights in a room next to the small lobby.

This was the kitchen—the biggest Danny had ever seen. He stared around at the counters, loaded with various gadgets and appliances, then at the huge refrigerator. Its door was covered with what looked like some kindergarten child's drawings and paintings.

"I bet those are Lester's," he said. "Josephine thinks the world of him."

"They sure aren't Vinnie's!" said Joe, with a chuckle. Then: "Uh-oh! Speak of the devil!"

Josephine and Lester's question-and-answer session had only just started up again. It faded almost at once.

Vinnie was standing at a far door that led to the rest of the house.

"Why don't you hurry up with some food, Josephine? I'm starved."

His smile was charming. The dimple was showing

to its best advantage. But the eyes behind those half-closed lashes were black and smoldering.

"Sure thing, Mr. Vinnie," said Josephine, getting into an apron. Her brownish yellow face was a mass of wrinkles, out of which the gentle brown eyes always seemed to be peering anxiously. Now the wrinkles deepened as she glanced at Vinnie. "I'm sorry. We were held up in traffic and—"

"That's OK," said Vinnie, with a chilly sniff. Then his expression changed. His lips parted in a smile that was almost genuine. "Hey, Lester—why don't you come and help me with a small problem while your grandmother's rustling up a meal?"

Lester's eyes brightened. There was nothing suspicious or anxious in his face as he looked at Vinnie.

"Sure, Mr. Vinnie! I'd be glad to!"

Josephine's expression became even more anxious as she watched Lester cross to the door. And as the ghosts followed Lester, Danny became aware that she too had started to follow, the moment Vinnie had gone out of her sight and was leading the way into a room farther along the corridor.

Danny hadn't time to see whether she was following them all the way, but once he and Joe had slipped into the book-lined room with Lester, he had the opportunity to check. Lester had left the door open behind him, and Vinnie was too intent on his "problem" to tell the boy to close it, or possibly even to notice.

"Watch this, Lester," he said, picking up the deck of cards.

He began to flip them into the corner of the room, where a large box lay on the floor.

"Sure, Mr. Vinnie," said Lester, looking puzzled, as one card after another skimmed into the corner, hitting the walls but missing the box.

"I'm trying to see how many cards I can flip into the box," said Vinnie, sliding a sideways glance at the boy. "But I don't seem to be having any luck, do I?"

"No, sir." Lester sounded sad.

"So what I want you to do, Lester, is hold the box for me. And move it around. And try to catch the cards if they look like they're going to miss. That way I should do better, right?"

The puzzled frown slowly cleared from Lester's face. Beyond the open door—as Danny could see—the suspicious frown cleared from Josephine's face at the same time. With no more than a lifting of the shoulders to betray a silent sigh, she tiptoed away. It obviously looked to her like what it looked to Danny and Joe: one more example of Vinnie's making things easy for himself. Even a stupid game like that!

"Yes, *sir*, Mr. Vinnie!" said Lester, moving slowly to pick up the box.

"Good! And Lester, you may call me Vinnie. Cut out the *mister*. All right?"

Lester stopped halfway to the box.

"But my gramma calls you Mr. Vinnie all the time."

"Yes. And she'd better! . . ." Vinnie forced the smile back to his face, no doubt seeing the look of alarm flash into Lester's. "No, Lester. That's different. She works here. But you—you're a visitor. And my friend."

The alarm had gone, but there was still a look of discomfort in Lester's eyes.

"But Gramma's your friend too, isn't she? She's everybody's friend. She—"

"Lester, the box. If you don't hurry, your grandma will have dinner ready and there won't be time for a game. Now, will there?"

"No, Mr. Vinnie."

Vinnie sighed as Lester picked up the box.

"What beats me is why he wants the kid to play at all," said Joe. "It seems like an even bigger pain, now that he has a partner."

But, as Lester turned, holding up the box, Vinnie's teeth flashed in a wide smile.

"That's great, Lester! Just a little lower. Good! ready?"

The first three cards were pretty accurate. Two went into the box, and one only just missed—and Lester hadn't even had to make a move.

"See what I mean?" said Vinnie. "I'm doing twice as good with you to help."

Lester grinned back, delighted.

"There's something wrong here," Joe muttered, staring at Vinnie's flicking fingers. "He's really trying now. He wasn't before."

"Yeah, but— Huh! *Now* he isn't trying."

Vinnie's aim had suddenly become erratic.

"Hey, come on, Lester!" he said, in a hurt tone. "Move it! You're supposed to be helping me. Catch them, why don't you?"

Lester nodded. He began to move the box from side to side, up and down. Once again, Vinnie's score started to improve. Lester yelled with triumph every time a card fell in the box, and groaned aloud whenever one missed. Vinnie increased the pace. Lester began to sweat—still crowing and groaning, still enjoying himself.

"Change the angle, Lester, change the way it's pointing!"

Lester, fumbling, tried to obey, shifting his grip on the box, moving his hands from one part to another, tilting it, lifting it—and finally dropping it.

"Gee! I'm sorry, Mr. Vinnie!"

"That's OK, Lester. Leave it there. Go see if your grandmother needs any help with the meal."

"But—"

"I said leave it!"

Vinnie's voice was hard and cold. Lester looked crestfallen as he went out of the room.

"Well, there was no need to snap at the kid like that!" said Danny. "What was there to get mad about?"

"Vinnie isn't mad," said Joe, quietly. "Not in the angry sense, anyway. Look at his eyes."

As Vinnie gazed down at the box and the spilled cards, a look of pure glee had crossed his face.

"I don't get it," said Danny. "What is there to be so *pleased* about, either?"

"I think I'm beginning to see," murmured Joe, stooping to get a closer look at the box, which had a covering of glossy gold-colored paper. "Oh, yes!" he said—and now he sounded very grim—"I think I'm beginning to see! Just take a look at him now!"

Vinnie had made no attempt to pick up the box so far. But he was still gazing down at it with a kind of black glittering triumph. And, as he did so, he slowly drew from a pocket a pair of gloves.

They were gray kid gloves. The pair he'd been wearing when spiking the chocolate.

He put them on again now.

Then he stooped to the box and, very carefully,

holding it as near its edges as possible, he picked it up.

"Thank you, Lester," they heard him murmur to himself. "Thank you for that fine set of sweaty fingerprints!"

"Wow!" gasped Danny, his eyes widening. Then: "The Devil's pasteboards!" he whispered.

"The Devil's what?" said Joe, as somewhere in another room a telephone started ringing.

"Oh, it was just something I thought about a few minutes ago. But really and truly, Joe, this guy is—"

Whatever it was that Danny thought Vinnie Boyars was didn't get spoken, because just then the telephone stopped ringing and Josephine's voice floated into the room.

"Mr. Vinnie! Telephone for you. It's Miss Jeanine, and she says to tell you it's urgent. She—uh—she sounds kinda scared."

9
The
Shadowy Shape

Karen and Carlos had no difficulty in getting into Jeanine's apartment building. It was one of the town's few high-rise structures, and although it was only a modest sixteen stories compared to the twenty or more floors in most big city high-rise buildings, it did have a doorman.

And that's what the two ghosts found most important.

It meant that they didn't have long to wait, when they arrived there shortly before 5:30. This was one of the doorman's busiest periods, with people coming home from work, and he was having to hold the door open two or three times every minute.

Nor did the pair have much trouble finding out Jeanine's apartment number. They both remembered Vinnie mentioning her surname, and that it was fairly long and began with Z—and that was plenty to go on. A quick check on the mailroom boxes showed that of the three people in the building whose names began with that letter, only one had the first initial *J*.

"That's it!" said Carlos, stabbing a finger at the name tag. "J. Zimmerman, 7F."

"Right!" said Karen. "So let's slip into the next upbound elevator and hope someone gets out at the seventh floor."

"Yeah, maybe even Jeanine herself!"

"If she's not home already. . . . Come on. There's someone stepping in the elevator now."

It wasn't Jeanine. It was a tall, weary-looking man. He sighed heavily as he punched the button for his floor. His two invisible companions groaned aloud. They'd drawn a 6, and the door had closed.

"I supposed we could get out and try the fire stairs," muttered Carlos, as the elevator slowed down.

"Stay where you are!" said Karen, grabbing him. "Haven't you ever been in one of these new buildings? The fire doors are so heavy it takes some *living* people all their strength to open them."

She was exaggerating, of course. But Carlos saw her point. A ghost—well, a ghost wouldn't stand a ghost of a chance! And since few people ever used the stairs in a building with elevators, the two uninvited visitors could be waiting outside one of those doors all night without having any luck.

"Looks like we're in for a long ride!" Carlos murmured, as the apparently empty elevator began its journey back to the lobby.

"Yes," said Karen. "The Yo-yo Express! . . . But we'll just have to be patient."

Patience wasn't one of Carlos's strong points. During the next three trips—to 15, 3 and 11—he kept himself entertained by wondering if a ghost might show up on the TV monitoring screens in the lobby—picked up by the camera's eye in the ceiling of the elevator. But he knew in his heart that no TV camera yet invented was sensitive enough for that—so that his waving up at the lens while pulling horrible faces was nothing more than a way of letting off steam.

"I wish you'd cut that out, Carlos!" said Karen, as they started out on their fourth trip—to 12—with a fat lady and a little girl.

"No one can see me!" said Carlos, glancing at their fellow passengers.

"No? What about me? I can. And it's getting on my nerves."

Carlos shrugged and rolled his eyes and sighed heavily. To tell the truth, Karen was beginning to get on *his* nerves, with her mother-hen fussing. And maybe, in their frustration, the two would have lapsed into outright bickering—if the next passenger up hadn't pressed the 7 button.

"Terrific!" said Carlos. "I told you we wouldn't have long to wait, didn't I?"

"You did? When—? Oh, never mind! Just be ready."

The elevator had come to a stop. The living passenger was an old man with a bad-tempered face. He pressed the OPEN DOOR button impatiently when the door failed to open at once. But when he did start getting out, he took his time, holding the door open with his shoulder while he juggled with his attaché case and a sack of groceries.

It didn't take them long to find which way the letters on the doors ran. Apartment 7F was to their right, almost at the end. They were a little thrown for a spell, when they found the grouchy old man was following them, but he stopped short at 7E and let himself in there.

"I was beginning to think his name might be Jedidiah Zimmerman and we'd made a big mistake," said Carlos, laughing—happy again, now he was back on the scent.

But there was still one more trial for him.

Inside 7F, all was silent.

"Looks like she isn't home yet," he said, dolefully.

"Yes," said Karen. "Good!"

"Huh?"

"Sure! If she *was* in, and she didn't plan on going out tonight, and she didn't have any visitors, we might never get in. This way, all we have to do is wait until she comes."

Carlos worked off his impatience this time by prowling up and down the corridor, studying the names on the doors, and peeping into the laundry room, before going back to the elevator door and listening. There he would soon begin to jig from foot to foot as he heard the car coming and watched the numbers change on the little indicator—only to groan and pretend to tear his hair as the car went on up, to 8 or 9 or beyond.

Karen smiled wearily and tried to settle down to think what they might do, once the woman returned. But her companion kept distracting her.

"Carlos! For heaven's sakes!" she called out, when he let out an especially piercing groan, after he'd heard

the elevator slow down and set his hopes soaring—
only to stop at 6.

"I can't help it! I—ah! Hey! It's continuing up *here!*
It's slowing again. It's—she's *here!*"

The elevator had stopped. The door rumbled open.

Karen heard the woman first, heard her voice say
to someone still inside, "Excuse me," then, "Come on!"

And out she stepped, with a rattling of chains, steel
and gold, the dog's and her own, with Carlos prancing in front of her, his eyes sparkling, hurrying to join
Karen by the door.

But—

"Dana! Come *on!* Whatever's gotten into you?"

Jeanine had been pulled up short by the dog. The
animal had planted itself firmly on the carpet, growling. The woman cast a nervous glance into the laundry room.

"Come *on,* you silly dog! There's no one in there."

But Dana was staring straight ahead—seemingly at
the blank end wall of the corridor, just beyond the
door of 7F.

"It's us she's growling at," said Karen, whispering
in spite of the fact that no living person could have
heard her.

Dana seemed to have, though. The dog gave a
strange, strangled bark, part whimper.

"I just don't understand this at all, Dana! You're
usually so quiet and gentle. Now be a good dog and
come on."

"She isn't the only one who doesn't understand it,"
murmured Karen. "I'm glad *all* dogs don't react to us
like this."

Dana was now allowing herself to be inched along the carpet toward them. She had stopped growling but continued to whimper and cringe, and when she raised her head it was to sniff anxiously, then whimper again.

"I think I know what it is," said Carlos. "Those animals that can see and hear us—and it's individuals, not any special kind or breed—I've known cats to act like this—well—I think what bugs them is they can't *smell* us. Because even ghosts can't really smell other ghosts, even though they think they can, sometimes. Well, to an animal that lives by its sense of smell, that must be real spooky."

Something about Carlos's tone, low and even, and maybe the fact that he was looking at Karen while he spoke, must have reassured the dog a little. Enough, at any rate, for it to let Jeanine tug it gently toward the door, then to wait, with flattened ears, while she unlocked it.

But the moment Jeanine and Dana stepped inside, quickly followed by Carlos and Karen, the dog set up a great commotion again, growling and barking and bristling. She was backing off all the time, even when Carlos approached her with the friendliest of murmurs.

"Leave her, Carlos!" said Karen. "Leave her be. Let's take a look around in the other rooms, then maybe she'll settle down and get used to us."

Carlos nodded and straightened up.

"Yeah!" He sighed. "If only we could spook the woman the way we spook the dog."

"Well, maybe we can find a way, if we look carefully enough."

The first impression they received when they wandered through into the other rooms—the bathroom and the bedroom—leaving Jeanine to coax the dog into the kitchen and start opening cans—was one of complete chaos.

"I mean, just *look* at it!" said Karen. "Every surface crowded with odds and ends, drawers gaping open, clothes spilling out, the floor littered with towels, make-up jars, old magazines, loaded ashtrays—you name it! It looks like she'd had burglars!"

"Maybe she has!" said Carlos.

"No way!" said Karen. "It was like this in the living room. But she didn't turn a hair. She must be the messiest woman in the whole state!"

"Suits me," murmured Carlos. "There should be plenty of objects just crying out to be tipped over and onto the floor in a place like this."

"Huh!" Karen grunted, gazing around with wrinkled nose. "Looks like they're dropping on the floor all the time, without any help from ghosts. She'd never even notice, I bet."

"Let's see what it's like in the kitchen, anyway. Maybe if we could get something to fall with a real loud crash—"

But the only really loud noise they created in there—among all the dirty pots and pans and the four dishes left on the floor, with half-eaten food on them—was the barking of Dana.

"Oh, for heaven's sakes!" wailed Jeanine, when this latest bout triggered off a hammering on the neighboring wall. "Come on, Dana. You're going to bed. Perhaps you'll settle down in there."

Grabbing the dog's collar, she tugged it, still growling and whimpering, in the direction of the bedroom.

"Looks like she's cracking already," said Carlos. "Why don't we go and concentrate on the dog?"

"No!" Karen shook her head. "Stay here. If she takes it in there, she'll probably shut the door on it. Then we'd be cut off from her. And it's *her*, remember, who's our target. She's the one who's prepared to go along with Vinnie's plot. We can't take it out on some poor innocent animal."

Carlos nodded.

"You're right," he said. Then he brightened. Jeanine was returning to the living room, after shutting the bedroom door, just as Karen had predicted. "Look at her hands. She's *really* shook up!"

The woman was lighting a cigarette. Or trying to. At the fourth or fifth attempt, she managed it. Then, breathing out a big plume of smoke, she cleared herself a space at the end of a heavily littered couch, sat down, and began to stare at the phone on a nearby table.

"She's wondering whether to phone a veterinarian, I bet," said Carlos.

"Or Vinnie," said Karen. "She's feeling so upset, she wants some sympathy. I know the feeling well."

Carlos raised his eyebrows, but said nothing. Suddenly, he clutched Karen's arm.

"Hey! *You're* pretty good at using your energy to make shapes, aren't you?"

"Sure!" Karen shrugged. "Out of fog, or swarms of gnats—stuff like that."

"Well, then!"

"Well *what*, then? I don't see any fog or gnats in here."

"Oh, no? How about cigarette smoke? What's that but a kind of fog? Or smog? Particles of carbon—suspended in gases."

Karen stared at the smoking woman. Jeanine was still gazing at the telephone, obviously thinking hard, taking deep drags at the cigarette and slowly letting out the plumes and jets of smoke. The smoke was then dispersing slowly around the rest of the room, rising as it did so.

But there was a point, somewhere between the couch and the reading lamp opposite, where it seemed to hang for a while, before continuing its upward drift.

"I could give it a whirl," said Karen, walking across to that point.

"OK, but wait until she lights this next one," said Carlos. "Then you should have some more material to work on."

The woman was already lighting another cigarette from the butt of the first. Then she stubbed out the butt in an overflowing ashtray, spilling some old butts onto the floor. She began taking deep thoughtful drags again.

The spilled butts were ignored. The smoke pall thickened around Karen.

Slowly, Karen closed her eyes. She stood very still. Carlos found himself tensing up in sympathy, knowing the tremendous effort his friend was preparing to put into this, as she mustered the energy, ready to focus it in one short all-out burst.

Jeanine was still staring absently through the smoke, turning something over in her mind.

Then the smoke—barely perceptibly at first—began to thicken around Karen's head and shoulders. Thicken and thicken, until Karen's features began to blur, as if she were wearing some filmy mask, or a beekeeper's veil. Thicken and thicken, until the smoke took on the shape of a human body, the shadow of a shape of the upper half of a human body.

Suddenly, Jeanine gave a little shriek and sat up straight. The ashtray fell from her lap. She rubbed her eyes. The dog in the next room responded with a loud barking. Someone knocked on a wall.

But seconds before that, Karen had emerged from the pall with a loud "Pow!"—as if she'd been holding her breath. And then there was only the drifting smoke to be seen—slightly wavering, the way smoke sometimes does in a draft.

Jeanine shook her head briskly, tried to laugh, but lapsed into a sob instead.

"Oh, shut *up*, Dana!" she called out.

Then she stumbled to the phone and dialed.

"Yes . . . yes. . . . I wish to speak with Vinn—with Mr. Vinnie Boyars. . . . Yes. Jeanine. Is that Josephine? . . . Oh, please hurry, Josephine! It's—tell him it's urgent!"

Karen and Carlos moved closer to the phone, putting their heads close to Jeanine's. The dog had quieted down.

"Do you think she saw me?" asked Karen.

"She certainly saw *something*," said Carlos. "Some shape."

Karen put a finger to her lips. Jeanine was speaking again.

"Oh, Vinnie, oh, I'm so glad you were in!"

"Well?" came Vinnie's hard drawl, out of the ear-piece.

"I—I don't know, but—well—I feel—I guess it's Dana—she's been acting so strangely. Like—like this afternoon, only worse."

"Have you thought of having her put to sleep? She *is* getting old, you know."

"Oh—but, Vinnie—I *couldn't.* . . . Besides, it isn't anything wrong with her. Not physically. I mean—well—this must sound crazy, but it's like some—someone—some real person was—was present. Only invisible. I mean invisible to me. But not to Dana."

"Have you been drinking?"

"Of *course* not! . . . Oh, Vinnie, I'm sorry! I didn't mean to snap. But it's getting so I—well, I could have sworn I saw someone's shadow."

A jeering laugh answered this.

"Come on, Jeanine! It isn't Halloween until Saturday night!"

"Oh, I know how it sounds, but—but, Vinnie—can you, would you come over tonight? Maybe have a bite to eat and—"

"No."

"No? But—"

"I'm busy. And I've already arranged to eat here."

Vinnie's voice, even over a phone that was at a distance from their ears, sounded cold and cruel to Karen and Carlos.

"Oh—well—I'm sorry!" Jeanine faltered. "I—I guess

I'm just a bit overwrought. It isn't that you're getting tired of me, though, Vinnie, is it?"

"Would I let you into my secrets if I were?"

That seemed to cheer the woman up. She snuffled and tittered—and at once forfeited every scrap of sympathy the others had started to feel for her.

"No! Of course you wouldn't! . . . Look, Vinnie, I'm sorry if I bothered you. . . . I—I feel tons better now. Just from hearing your voice. I guess I'll just settle down now. Wash my hair. Yes, that's what I'll do. I'll make myself look nice for you, ready for the party on Saturday."

"You do that" was Vinnie's dry reply. "Ciao!"

The line went dead.

As Jeanine dried her eyes and lit another cigarette, Karen sighed.

"If she's going to wash her hair, it looks like we're here for the night, whether we like it or not."

"Yeah!" said Carlos glumly. He knew what Karen meant. He had three sisters. Then he brightened. "Still, you have to admit, we've got her softened up. Now if only she's the type who has those special dreams, we might *really* get something to report to the others!"

10
The Decision

But Carlos and Karen didn't have anything like that to report, the following afternoon, when the full Ghost Squad met again as arranged.

"So *did* she have one of those dreams?" Buzz asked eagerly, when Carlos had reached this point in his account.

The word-processor screen remained blank for a few seconds. Then:

"We don't know. She might have. But—" The flickering faltered, before the message was resumed. *"Well, we just don't know."*

"What d'you *mean*, you don't know?" said Wacko.

"We didn't go into the bedroom to find out. Karen's decision. But I guess she was right. If we had gone in, then the dog would have barked all night and the woman wouldn't have slept at all. So we sat it out in the living room. There was no point in making the dog sick."

"It might have made the neighbors mad and gotten her into trouble that way," said Buzz, looking disappointed.

"He has a point there," Danny said to the other three.

Joe shook his head.

"No. Karen made the right decision. We're not trying to punish Jeanine for doing something wrong. We're trying to prevent something wrong from happening. And spooking Jeanine only seems to have brought her closer to Vinnie."

"Yes," said Carlos. "Because she was scared. But if we scared her even more, and she broke down—well, who knows?"

Joe still wasn't impressed.

"No," he said. "The only *effective* way of spooking them—and I mean scaring them off their plans for tomorrow—would be to let them know that real ghosts were watching them." He shrugged. "But that seems to be impossible."

He looked worried.

So did Wacko. Referring back to the word processor's last message, he said, "Anyway, what do we do next? We don't have much time, you know. Only a little over twenty-four hours."

Both he and Buzz were looking anxious as they turned to where they guessed the ghosts were standing. They had good cause to feel nervous.

The earlier reports had been equally unsatisfactory.

All that Joe's and Danny's had done had been to confirm how cunningly Vinnie was setting up his plans, and how bad it was beginning to look for Lester. The rest of their vigil hadn't yielded much, either.

Vinnie had spent most of the evening—after he'd taken Jeanine's call, and eaten his meal, and complained, probably unjustly, of its poor quality—lying on his bed with his door locked, watching some very nasty videotapes that specialized in torture. When he wasn't doing that, he was admiring his reflection in the mirror, practicing his smile, fingering his dimple. And when he finally retired, he slept like a baby, the smile still hovering on his lips. Whatever dreams *he* had, none of them was the type the two ghosts could butt in on.

As for Buzz and Wacko, they had learned that the senator wasn't leaving Brussels until early afternoon the following day, European time. Also that he'd be arriving at Kennedy Airport somewhere around four, and that he'd be driving straight home to keep his appointment with the trick-or-treaters and TV cameras.

"So he has one very tight schedule, as you may imagine," the secretary had said. "Was your business all that urgent?"

At the other end of the line, Wacko licked his lips.

"Very!" For a moment, he'd toyed with the idea of explaining everything. Then he realized how he'd almost certainly be regarded as a hoaxer or nut. Anyone who didn't know Vinnie and his viciousness really well would never believe their story. No. There was only one person who might take them seriously. "Is there any way of contacting the senator in Brussels? Tonight, perhaps? Some phone number where I can reach him?"

The woman sounded rueful.

"No way! He has a terribly crowded schedule, as I just told you. Even *we* haven't been able to get hold of him for the past day and a half. Sorry!"

"Well?" said Buzz, as he turned in his chair. "What do we do now?"

"Shall we try the police, after all?" said Wacko.

"*Grogan?*" flickered the screen.

"Why not?" said Wacko. "At least he'll remember that first time, when he wouldn't believe us until it was nearly too late."

"Yeah," said Buzz. "Maybe he won't be so quick to give us the brush-off this time." Suddenly he looked worried. "By the way, speaking of the Hyman case—have you seen Roscoe anywhere around?"

"*Negative,*" came the answer. Then: "*About Grogan—yes. Joe says to go ahead. It's all we can do for now.*"

"Right!" said Buzz. "We'll call him now. There's no point in sitting around when—"

"*No!! Hold it!*"

Buzz and Wacko stared at the screen. Buzz had already been getting to his feet. He sat down again.

"But—"

"*If you call the police out of the blue, and it isn't an immediate emergency, you could get stalled. Grogan is the only cop who's at all likely to give you a hearing. So go see him personally. Both of you. Now.*"

"Will he be in?" Wacko. "I mean—"

"*You won't know until you try, will you?*"

The transmission of the message was made by Carlos, of course.

But the words—and their tone—were Joe's.

The leader of the Ghost Squad was getting rattled. He'd been thinking of that golden box again, with its tempting but terrible contents.

11
The Strange Happenings in Detective Grogan's Office

Joe's hunch had been right. When Buzz and Wacko had announced to the desk sergeant that they had some important information for Detective Grogan, the man looked at them as if they'd just crawled out from under the floorboards. But when they insisted, telling the desk sergeant that they had once given the detective some information that had helped to thwart an armed robbery, he relented and picked up the phone.

"Gene? Coupla kids here say they have some important information for you. D'you want to see them now?"

They heard a rapid, rasping voice saying something in reply.

Wacko glanced at Buzz and rolled his eyes.

It sounded like Detective Eugene Grogan was in a bad mood.

"Well—uh—they didn't say," replied the sergeant. "All they said was that they'd helped you out before. And that their tip-off turned out to be the real McCoy. . . . Yeah—uh—" He glanced at the note he'd scribbled on his blotter. "Robert—uh—Phillips and Henry Williams."

This time, they heard the detective's actual words— "OK. Show 'em in"—and the weary tone in which those words were uttered.

Detective Grogan looked up from the pile of paperwork on his desk: forms, files and a stack of what looked like fingerprint records. He had sparse sandy hair, a beaky nose and a wide thin-lipped mouth.

"Well? What is it this time?" he said.

There was also a bottle of indigestion tablets on the desk. He reached for this now, tipped a couple of tablets into the palm of his hand and transferred them to his mouth.

"We have reason to believe—" Wacko began, somewhat tentatively.

Buzz took over.

"We know for *certain* that someone is preparing to spike some Halloween candy with old phonograph needles. The steel kind."

Grogan had been slowly champing the tablets. His jaws went still.

"Really?" He settled back in his chair, a faint gleam of interest in his eyes. "Some school-kid you know? Tell me more. Give me some facts. Then we'll see."

The look in his eyes seemed to add: "And those facts had better be *hard* facts!"

"Well," Wacko began, giving his lower lip a swift nervous lick, "I—we—"

82

"Like first," said Grogan, lurching forward and picking up a pen, "who is this person? And why is he doing it? And who does he intend the candy for? The facts."

Buzz cleared his throat.

"Well, sir, he's not really a school-kid. He's about twenty, twenty-one, which makes it worse. His name is Vinnie Boyars and—"

Detective Grogan had been scribbling notes and champing on his pills. But at the mention of Vinnie's name, he flung down his pen.

"Hey! Now wait!" he rasped, causing little flecks of white to form at his mouth corners. "Just hold it! You're not by any chance talking about that son of Senator Boyars, are you?"

"His stepson—yes," said Buzz.

"And this candy he's planning to spike—?"

"He's already spiked it, sir," said Wacko. "It's candy for the senator's party tomorrow night. . . ."

The detective listened in silence as Wacko outlined what they knew about the plot. Toward the end, Grogan closed his eyes tight, as if in pain, and began nodding impatiently.

"All right, all right!" he said, before Wacko had completely finished. "There's one big question I now have to ask." His eyes opened and flashed each of the boys a very fierce caution. "How come you know all this? Did the subject tell you himself?"

"No, sir."

There was another flash—this time of annoyance—when it became clear that Wacko wasn't about to add anything right then. That he was, in fact, looking uncertainly at Buzz instead.

"Did he tell someone *else* about this?" Grogan said, slowly and ominously. "And did that someone else tell you?"

"Well—uh—not exactly, sir," said Buzz.

The detective shut his eyes tight again. His hand reached out for the tablets. Then he seemed to recall that he'd only just taken a couple. He opened his eyes, and they looked cold and miserable—and mean.

"All right—so was it something that passed from person to person several times before it reached you? If so"—Grogan picked up his pen—"I shall need to have the name of the last person in this chain." He was obviously trying hard to speak patiently. "Before it reached yourselves, of course."

"Well, no, sir," said Buzz. "You've got it—uh—I mean, there was no chain of that kind. It isn't just a rumor. We *know*. . . . But look, if you don't believe us, why don't you go up there and challenge Vinnie?" At this point, Wacko had put out a restraining hand to Buzz's sleeve. Buzz shook it off. "Or at least go and ask the senator himself, when he gets back, to check that box of candy before he starts handing it out?"

Wacko sighed. He'd already guessed what was coming next.

"Wait a minute! Wait a minute!" Grogan had closed his eyes again. "You're asking *me*, a state employee, to go telling a state senator that his grown-up son is—"

He broke off and shook his head briskly, as if the pain had returned. Then he opened his eyes. Wide.

"*You!*" he said, stabbing a finger at Wacko. "*You're* embarrassed, I can tell. Your father is also a state em-

84

ployee and a very fine lawyer. *You* should know better. In fact, you *do* know better." He took a deep breath. "All right, so *you*, Henry Williams, you tell me who told you about this. Then I might—just *might*—go question that person. OK?"

There was a pause. Wacko's forehead was all creased up. Now he too seemed to be in pain. Then his forehead cleared, and he lifted his head and looked the detective straight in the eyes.

"Sorry, sir. We—we just can't tell you that. But it's absolutely true, and if you have a Holy Bible in here, I'm prepared to swear—"

"Now stop right there! I'm beginning to get the picture." Grogan slowly turned to Buzz, and the cold gray eyes came to rest on Wacko's friend like naval guns on a target that was soon to be blasted out of existence. "*You*—*you've* been dreaming again. Right? You've been picking up psychic messages again. Right?"

This was so near to the truth that, as Buzz began an attempt at a reply, he couldn't help smiling faintly.

"Well, sir, it—"

The smile obviously infuriated the man. The gray eyes blazed. He opened fire.

"Now hear this! I'm giving you five seconds to tell me the name or names of the person or persons who witnessed this young man placing dangerous substances inside articles of food, with intent to cause grievous bodily harm. And if you fail to tell me in those five seconds, I will seriously have to consider charging you—both of you—with wasting the time of a police officer on duty. OK? . . . OK! Five—four—three—"

"But, sir!" cried Buzz. "You said all this that other time. Remember? When we told you about those two hoods who were planning to knock off the Hyman jewelry store. And we were right, then—dead right— no matter how we came to hear about it, or who told us, or—or even if it *was* a psychic message."

Grogan's eyes had wavered. Wacko saw his chance to press home their case.

"In fact," he said, "you got yourself commended by the governor for stopping the robbery at the last minute."

Then something happened.

Up to this point, Grogan had been looking less irritable, more thoughtful. After all, what the boys were reminding him of was the truth. But all at once, his manner changed. He looked startled.

"What—?" He glanced over his shoulder and reached out toward the air conditioner, which was turned off. He shivered. "For a second or two there, I could have sworn that thing switched itself on." Then he shrugged and turned back to the boys. "Go on. You were saying about the Hyman incident. Are you telling me that the same person who tipped you off then—a person who for some reason insisted on remaining anonymous—are you telling me that this person is the present informant? The same one who told you about the perpetrators Kelly and Roscoe, and— What's the matter?"

The detective was looking up at Wacko, who had just given a convulsive start and was now rubbing his neck and looking around.

"I—I thought I felt a draft of cold air. Only not from

there"—he nodded at the air conditioner—"but from the door."

Grogan shrugged. A sour smile crept over his lips.

"Ever since we moved into this new building, we've been having trouble. If it isn't drafts, it's—*now* what?"

Buzz was bending down, frantically rubbing his right leg, just below the knee.

"No—it's nothing, sir." Buzz straightened up. He hardly liked to mention the fact that he too had felt the same strange coolness—this time low down, and from an entirely different direction. He was afraid that Detective Grogan might start to think they were mocking him. And besides that, he was beginning to wonder just what might be causing these sensations. Joe and the others hadn't actually said they would be coming along to the police station with them. But if Buzz knew anything about the other four, and their growing anxiety, he'd have been willing to bet everything he'd got on the fact that they were here now. "I just got an—ouch!—I—I mean an itch!"

What had caused him to jump like a startled cat was a sudden vibration in his left shoulder—a sudden shuddering shaking—accompanied again by the strange faint chilliness. It was a sensation he'd never felt in his life before. It couldn't have lasted for more than three seconds, but Buzz knew right then it was something he'd never forget for the rest of his life—no matter how long he lived.

"S-sorry, sir!" he said, fighting to control his voice, bracing every muscle in his body against any further shocks. "We were telling you how right we'd been that other time, when that guy Roscoe, the one you shot, and his accomplice—"

This time Detective Grogan himself appeared to have been the target. He'd jumped up from his chair, done a 180-degree turn and made a grab at the air conditioner—all in one movement. He ran the palm of his hand over the vents. There was a frown on his face. It was a frown of perplexity rather than annoyance.

"Maybe there's some intermittency in the motor of this thing, and it really does keep turning itself on," he muttered. Then he sat down again and forced a sardonic grin. "Or I guess *you'd* say it was something psychic, something connected with the spirit world!"

Buzz didn't say anything to this. If he had, it would have been a resounding, *"Yes! I sure would!"*

He glanced anxiously at Wacko. Wacko was looking equally disturbed.

Just what *was* going on in that office?

12
The Fight

During the debate the day before, Buzz and Wacko had been quite accurate in their descriptions of what happens when ghosts touch living people. But only up to a point.

It was true, for example, that a living person—if he or she feels anything at all—is conscious only of the slightest coolness, like the brush of a fly or a tiny particle of moisture. It was also true that even if a ghost deliberately hits a living person, it will still only register as a slight coolness.

But what the two boys didn't know—because it was such a rare occurrence that Carlos and the others hadn't thought to tell them—was this:

When the contact between a ghost and a living person is prolonged beyond the fraction of a second taken up by a normal touch or blow—as in clutching or squeezing or hug-

ging—the results are somewhat different. The coolness itself becomes prolonged, and is accompanied by a sense of vibration in some cases. Especially where extraordinarily massive quantities of psychic energy are involved.

Generally, ghosts know better than to try to affect the living in that way. For one thing, it can't be kept up without seriously affecting the ghost. He or she experiences a warm, sickening, lurching sensation, quickly followed by a draining of energy.

So even Malevs rarely attempt to attack the living by such direct means, knowing that the limited effects on the living aren't worth the damage to themselves—the drain and the unpleasantness. And all ghosts, whether Malevs or not, usually go out of their way to avoid *accidental* prolonged contact with the living. In this, they are aided by a split-second early-warning system of reflexes, almost like radar, which enables them to sidestep such contact.

But when ghosts are fighting each other—actually coming to grips and blows—that's a different matter.

When a ghost fights another ghost, desperately or savagely—knowing that real injury can be inflicted just as if they were two living people—each of them is far too preoccupied by this conflict even to think of avoiding any living bystanders. How could it be otherwise, especially in the case of a defending ghost, when his body is being pushed or dragged or knocked off balance by his assailant?

Which is how it was in Detective Grogan's office that afternoon . . .

Buzz had been right in *his* hunch, too. The four ghosts hadn't been able to resist accompanying the two boys on their visit to the police station.

"You never know," Joe said. "We may be able to help them in some way."

"Yeah!" said Carlos. "Like if they get the brush-off and someone tells them Grogan is out on a case when he's really in his office, we can alert them and get them to persist."

"Correct," said Joe. "Only unless something like that *does* arise, let's not keep touching them to show we're around. It might fluster them, and if my guess is right, they're going to need all their concentration."

"What d'you mean?" said Karen.

"*I* know," said Danny, rather gloomily. "To convince Grogan, right, Joe?" When Joe nodded, Danny went on. "I mean, I know Grogan from when I was alive. The time when I'd dreamed about a robbery that was going to take place, and we tried to warn him."

"Yes, of course," said Karen. "I forgot. That's why he gets so leery about Buzz—thinking it's some ESP nonsense again."

"It *wasn't* nonsense!" said Danny. "It—"

"Cut it out, you two!" said Joe. "Just be ready to go into that office when *they* go in."

At that point, the ghosts were standing right behind the boys as they were talking to the desk sergeant. But when Buzz and Wacko were shown into Grogan's office, they relaxed a little. The department believed in an open-door policy, unless an officer was engaged in some very serious and confidential discussion, and obviously Buzz and Wacko didn't rate that treatment. The door was already open when they arrived, and it was left open after they'd been shown into the room.

"Well, at least he's agreed to see them," said Carlos, when the detective began questioning Buzz and Wacko.

"Yes, but not very graciously!" said Karen.

"Be quiet and listen!" said Joe.

They listened intently at first, watching every line on the detective's face and every small, seemingly casual movement he made. Being ghosts didn't mean they could read people's thoughts, any more than they could have when they were alive. But at the same time, being ghosts meant that their perceptions were sharper. They usually didn't have to bother about anybody watching *their* reactions. They didn't feel such minor distractions as bugs, or pangs of indigestion, or rumbling bowels, or creeping headaches. Or have background worries about the time, and catching trains or buses. Such big, looming topics as money or health didn't worry them at all.

In short, they didn't have any of the conflicting thoughts or feelings that usually nag at the living, causing lapses in concentration. As a result, they were able to read people's faces and gestures so accurately that sometimes it really did seem that they were reading their minds.

"He's buying it," said Joe, when Grogan picked up his pen and began making notes. "He's definitely interested."

"Let's hope he stays that way," muttered Danny, doubtfully. "I mean—"

"Oh, boy!" Karen groaned.

That was when Grogan flung down his pen at the mention of Vinnie Boyars.

"That's done it!" said Carlos, equally despairing.

"Not so fast," said Joe. "It's thrown him a little, yes. But he still wants to know more."

"Yes, but they haven't reached the *really* tricky part yet," said Danny. "There's no way they can tell him the real truth, that they're in *direct* contact with a bunch of ghosts!"

When Grogan finally opened up on Buzz and started talking about dreams and psychic messages, Danny sighed.

"There you are! What did I tell you? Now he'll have them thrown out."

"I wonder what they *will* say, though," murmured Karen, as Grogan started his countdown. "How will they handle it?"

"Buzz won't crack, anyway," said Danny, glancing admiringly at his old friend, and the way he wasn't flinching.

"Wacko won't, either!" snapped Carlos, glancing at *his* old friend. "He might bend, but he'll never—"

And that's when the trouble *really* began.

Buzz had just started to remind Grogan of the attempted jewelry heist, and he'd no sooner uttered the words, "When we told you about those two hoods who were planning to knock off the Hymans' jewelry store"—than there came a howl of rage from the far corner of the room, and a dark-clad figure leaped out from the shadows behind a big filing cabinet.

The four ghosts were taken completely by surprise. They'd been so intent on listening to the conversation and studying Grogan's face that they simply hadn't bothered to look in any other part of the office.

"So it was *you* jerks!" growled the figure, pausing momentarily in a deep crouch, where his first spring had landed him. "It was *you* and—and *them!*"

"It's Roscoe!" said Karen, in a dry whisper.

Roscoe's eyes blazed as he glanced at Buzz and Wacko.

"What—?" Joe fought to control his voice. It was obvious to him that Roscoe had heard enough of both conversations—the one between the living and the parallel one between the ghosts—to have guessed at least a part of the truth. Joe decided to play for time. "What are *you* doing here?" he said, trying to sound only mildly concerned.

"What d'ya think?" Roscoe's low, growling snarl was chilling even to their ears. "What better place to hang around—huh? In—in the hope of finding out who blew the whistle on ya?" Roscoe was having difficulty with his breathing, too. His crouch was deepening even further. "Well, now I *know!*" he screamed, springing straight for Carlos.

Whether it was because Carlos was the nearest, or whether it was because he was the smallest, they never did find out. Maybe Roscoe—realizing that Joe was bigger than he, and that it was four against one, anyway—had some notion of grabbing Carlos as a hostage. On the other hand, he looked too mad with fury to have worked out any sort of plan like that in so short a time.

Whatever Roscoe's intention, it was lucky for Carlos that Joe's reflexes were very quick. In one swift movement, the leader of the Ghost Squad had grabbed

Carlos and flung him out of harm's way and taken his place at the end of Roscoe's spring. This meant that Joe was not as well set as he might have been, and it made him fall off balance, with Roscoe's hands already grappling for his throat.

That was when—as the struggling bodies reeled against him, and Joe was held there for a few seconds, fighting to break the Malev's grip—Detective Grogan made his first complaint about the air conditioner.

"You three stand back!" Joe yelled when he'd managed to free his neck. "Leave him to me!"

He was aiming to get Roscoe in an armlock. But the Malev was fighting back like a tiger, spitting and snarling, and, despite his smaller size, he flung Joe halfway across the room, straight into Wacko, following up immediately with another spring and another attempt at a stranglehold.

That was when *Wacko* complained of the draft.

Joe went down under the sheer fury of that onslaught, wrenching his neck this way and that, to try to avoid those steely clawlike fingers. But Roscoe persisted. It was as if those hands had independent indestructible minds of their own. And in the next few seconds, they'd found their target again, and secured it.

"Oh! Oh, *no!*" cried Karen. "He—he's choking Joe to death!"

Nobody smiled, then or at any other time. They knew only too well that ghosts do have lives to lose. And that other ghosts are perfectly capable of taking those lives.

Joe's face was turning blue. His breath was coming

in dreadful wheezing rasps. The two locked bodies rolled across the floor.

That was when Buzz felt the sensation in his right leg.

But suddenly, with one last desperate burst of energy, Joe managed to jab Roscoe with his knee, right in the groin. The hands relaxed their grip as the Malev, grunting with pain, recoiled. He tried to get to his feet, and nearly made it, as Joe lunged forward, still on his knees, trying to follow up with a kind of makeshift football tackle.

As Roscoe began to go down, he clutched at Buzz's shoulder.

It was useless, of course, as far as gaining any support was concerned. Either Roscoe was too new as a ghost to know any better or he was simply too hard-pressed to be capable of thinking what he was doing.

At any rate, that was when Buzz experienced the terrible three-second sensation that he was to remember all his life.

And it might even have lasted longer. But Joe, with blood already oozing from his neck, wasted no time. Grabbing Roscoe with his left hand, he yanked the Malev toward him while simultaneously hitting him hard with his right fist.

As Joe's fist made contact with Roscoe's chin, the crack was so loud that it made some of the others gasp and wonder that even the living didn't hear it.

But still Roscoe wasn't subdued. He staggered back, eyes looking dazed but still murderous. Then, just at that moment, Buzz mentioned him again, by name, saying how he'd been shot by Grogan—the man sitting there, just inches away!—and the murderousness flared up, once more full strength.

This time, however, Roscoe made the mistake of directing this murderous energy straight at a living person—something no seasoned Malev would ever have attempted, no matter how great his lust for revenge. With a screech of rage, he made a grab at Grogan's throat from behind.

That was all Joe needed. He took one step forward and launched a swinging chop to the side of Roscoe's head, just behind the left ear.

Then, as Grogan got up to feel the air conditioner, they watched Roscoe slowly sink to the floor and—disappear.

It was instantaneous. Roscoe's knees had barely reached the rug, his hands still groping for some kind of support, when he simply vanished.

The ghosts weren't as astonished as they might have been, had they been as new to ghosthood as Roscoe. They themselves had disappeared like that from time to time, and seen each other disappear, on the rare occasions when they'd fallen asleep. Then, as they knew, a ghost would vanish for days at a time, only to reappear again in exactly the same spot, completely oblivious to what had happened in the meantime.

It was a strange phenomenon, and usually very inconvenient, but they were used to it.

This time, however . . .

"Joe," said Karen, in a subdued voice, as their leader dabbed gingerly at his neck, "do—do you think—I mean, have you *killed* him?"

Joe frowned thoughtfully. He shook his head.

"I doubt it. He's just been knocked out. I've seen it happen before. It's like going to sleep, but it doesn't last as long. He'll be back, all right!" he added grimly. "Maybe in a few hours. Certainly by tomorrow."

"So—where does that leave us?" said Danny.

"In trouble," said Joe. He glanced around. The phone had just begun to ring. The detective was picking it up. "Let's just hope that these two have managed to convince Grogan while we've been so—uh—preoccupied. Then at least we'll be able to concentrate on our own safety."

But they were to have no such break.

"OK. I'll be right there," Grogan was saying into the receiver. Then: "You two—out! That was a real live emergency, and I don't have any more time to waste on kids' dreams!"

"But—"

"You heard what I said!" The detective was already reaching for his coat. "Leave! *Now!*"

"Come on, Buzz," Wacko murmured. "We'd better talk it over with the others. We're wasting time here."

"Yeah!" said Carlos, as they followed the boys out. "And that wasn't the only thing that nearly got wasted!"

He was thinking of Roscoe's first leap, and of whom the target had been then, and wondering whether he—Carlos Gomez—would be so lucky next time.

13
Vinnie's Late-Night Ceremony

This new and terrible crisis was uppermost in everyone's mind when the Ghost Squad met again in Wacko's room, shortly after the interview with Grogan. Buzz and Wacko had been aghast when—in answer to Buzz's semijoshing question, "Hey, you guys! What were you doing in there? It felt like you were breakdancing!"—Carlos gave them a full account over the screen.

Wacko gulped.

"Oh, boy!" he murmured. "So what d'you think he'll do next? When he—uh—wakes up?"

"Well, he won't tangle with Joe again, that's for sure!" Carlos answered bravely, trying to fight down his own fears.

But Joe made him—and all the others—face the truth.

"Maybe not," he said. "But what he might do—what he very likely *will* do—is try to pick off the weaker members, one at a time. Like Karen, and Danny—and you."

Carlos nodded miserably.

"I'd already figured that out myself!"

"So tell Buzz and Wacko that. But tell them that *they* shouldn't worry too much. Not for the first week or so, anyway. Until he gets more experience, there's very little Roscoe can do to harm *them*. So, for the next twenty-four hours, it'll be safe for them to concentrate on the main problem. How to stop Vinnie."

After Carlos had passed this on, Buzz and Wacko were still troubled.

"But what if—?" Buzz broke off and turned to the space in front of the word processor. "Sorry, Carlos, but I have to remind you all of this." He turned back to where he imagined Joe and the others were. "What if Roscoe manages to kidnap—or—or even *kill*—Carlos? The Ghost Squad itself would be as good as finished then, wouldn't it? I mean the whole operation—us included."

"Tell them," said Joe, "that we are only too well aware of that. And that from now on—until something's done about Roscoe—the four of us will go everywhere together. There'll be no more splitting up, except in extreme emergencies or other very special circumstances."

"You bet!" said Carlos, brightening up as he began to transmit this message. . . .

"So now," said Joe, when Buzz and Wacko had read it in gloomy silence, "let's get down to the main business. Time's running out fast, and apparently we can't count on any help from Grogan."

They wrestled with the problem for over half an hour, without anyone coming even close to a solution. Mrs. Williams was beginning to sound impatient as she shouted up the stairs to tell Wacko he wouldn't be eating *at all* that evening, if he didn't come down soon—and wasn't it time his friend was heading home, too?

"*OK,*" the screen flickered. "*Here's what we do. We four will have one more try to spook Vinnie, or Jeanine, or both.*"

"Without splitting up this time, I hope!" said Wacko.

"*You bet without spliting up! And even if we don't spook either of them, at least we might pick up on some new angle, just by being around them all night. And Joe says since it's Saturday tomorrow, we can report earlier. How about 9:30 in the morning?*"

"Suits me," said Buzz, glancing at Wacko.

"Sure," said Wacko. "But let's hope you have something useful to tell us. Even if it's only something useful for Buzz and me to be doing. Because by then there'll only be about nine hours left."

Possibly—if the ghosts had been able to split up the way they had the previous night—they would have had better luck. Possibly not.

As it was, they wasted over three hours in Jeanine's building, most of it in the corridor outside her silent apartment.

"Could be she isn't coming back at all tonight," said Karen, when they heard a clock strike ten in the old man's apartment next door. "Could be she's gone away for the weekend."

"Could be she's gone away *forever!*" said Carlos, thinking of Jeanine's nervousness the night before. "Moved out for good."

He looked absolutely miserable, having felt himself dying a second death for the past two hours, this time of sheer impatience.

It was Danny who delivered the final blow to their spirits.

"What if she's been with Vinnie all evening?"

"I know," said Joe, with a sigh. "That's just what I've been thinking. If we'd gone up there right away, instead of stopping off here first, just because it happened to be nearer to Wacko's house, we might have been with both of them right now!"

"Gosh, yes!" said Karen. "And I bet if we'd managed to spook her while Vinnie was present, he'd have gotten so mad they'd be fighting each other. Then we really might have had something to work on."

"How?" said Danny.

"Come on!" said Karen. "You've heard the saying about when thieves fall out. Well, the same goes for conspirators."

Danny shrugged.

"Yeah. But the way our luck's been running, if we *had* gone there first, the chances are that they'd both have been here. Or someplace else altogether."

Joe was frowning. He didn't like the sound of this. It had too much of the hollow ring of defeat for his liking. And in his view, ghosts had no business even *thinking* about luck, let alone counting on it.

Just then, a man and woman came around the corner at the far end of the corridor, calling out their good-nights to someone back there. When the man pressed the button for the elevator, Joe made up his mind.

"The way our *luck's* running," he said, repeating Danny's words scornfully, "this might be the last chance we'll have to get out of here tonight. So let's do some running of our own—something we *can* control—and go on to Vinnie's right away."

Up at the Boyars residence, they couldn't get indoors at all. It wasn't as eerie as the previous night. There were lights in several windows on the first and second floors. But the only one on the first floor without drapes or blinds of any kind was the kitchen. And the only person in there was Josephine, still toiling away between table and counter and stove. A row of small pies stood on a ledge just inside the window that the ghosts were looking through, the heat from the pies causing a slight shimmer.

"Looks like she's preparing extra food for tomorrow night's party," said Karen.

"Yeah," grunted Joe. The kitchen clock was coming up to eleven. Twenty hours to go. "Let's try again. See if we can get inside *somehow*."

They prowled around for a while, searching in vain for an open downstairs window, waiting in vain for someone to arrive or depart.

"I suppose Josephine took Lester home long before now," said Karen.

"Yeah," said Danny. "That's if he came here at all today. She was probably too busy to have him around."

The kitchen clock had registered 11:30, and they'd

watched Josephine take a final weary look around on her way out of the room, before Carlos spotted anything like a hopeful break.

"Along there!" he cried, tugging at Joe's sleeve. "See it? A light. A new one. Just gone on. Next to the corner room where Vinnie was playing his card game."

They ran along the side of the building, eager to get there before anyone drew the drapes. But they didn't need to worry. The person inside was either too preoccupied or too unconcerned at this late hour to bother with the window.

"It's Vinnie!"

"Wow! Just look at that robe!"

Vinnie was resplendent in a green silk dressing gown with black and yellow dragons.

"He looks somehow—*ceremonial!*" said Karen, in awe, remembering a movie she'd once seen, in which a Chinese warlord had spent the night before a cruel massacre offering up prayers.

But Vinnie wasn't offering up any prayers.

"Never mind what he's wearing," said Joe. "What's he *doing?* This looks like the senator's den."

It, too, was book lined, but it wasn't as big as the library, and there was a large desk instead of a table. What clinched it for Joe, however, was a picture on one of the side walls—a large framed photograph of Senator Boyars being sworn in.

Vinnie was gazing at it now, an ugly sneer on his face. The dimpled chin began to wag as he muttered something. Then the dragons writhed when he shot out a hand. It looked as if he were going to snatch that picture from the wall and stomp on it. But instead he felt behind it, where it was hooked to the wall, and pulled something out.

"It's a key!" said Carlos, as Vinnie walked across to a corner closet.

Then, as he unlocked the closet, they remembered what they'd overheard Vinnie telling Jeanine.

"He's going to help himself to a drink," murmured Joe. "Yes. Look."

They watched, as Vinnie filled a small glass from a fancy-looking bottle, swigged half its contents in one gulp, then took the rest over to the picture of the senator.

His face was flushed already. Whatever it was, the liquid must have been pretty strong. And when he raised his glass to the picture, they heard his words distinctly.

"Here's mud in your eye, you old jerk! And mud on your good name, too, by this time tomorrow!"

There was so much exultation in the words—so much evil exultation—that Karen shuddered.

"Ugh! He gives me the creeps!"

But she watched with the others as Vinnie went back to the closet, swilled his glass out at a small sink in there and put back in the bottle the same quantity of water as the liquid he'd just drunk.

"It's a wonder he doesn't do worse than that," muttered Danny. "It's a—"

He broke off, as Carlos gripped his arm and said, "Hey! Look what he's doing *now!*"

Vinnie had opened a small chest, under the drinks shelf. Taking a black silk handkerchief from the pocket of his robe, he used it to cover his fingers. Then he drew from the chest the same large gold-colored box they'd seen before. There was a peculiar gloating look on his face—almost an adoring look—as he gazed at the box for a few seconds, before carefully, even reverently, placing it back in the chest.

As Vinnie returned the key to its hiding place behind the picture, put out the light and left the room, Carlos was almost chattering with rage.

"The creep! The dirty rotten creep! If—if only we could break in and take that box and throw it in the river! It wouldn't be stealing! It would be doing a public service!"

"Hey, *yes!*" said Karen, suddenly clapping her hands. "Why not?" Then, just as suddenly, her shoulders slumped. "But no. It wouldn't be possible. Not in broad daylight."

"It wouldn't be possible anytime," said Joe. "Not for us."

"I wasn't thinking about us. I was thinking if push came to shove tomorrow, and there wasn't any other course left, Buzz and Wacko could do it."

"Do what?" said Joe, staring at her.

"Break in and get the chocolates. But of course, in broad daylight—"

"Are you out of your mind, girl?" said Joe. "Daylight or moonlight, we can't ask them to do *that!* Just think of the harm it would do them if they were caught. They—they've got their lives ahead of them, you know!"

"It was just a thought," murmured Karen, hanging her head a little. Then her hair flew as she lifted her face defiantly. "But we have to think of *something!* We can't let this—this horrible plot succeed!"

14
The Second Bird

When Carlos mentioned this idea of Karen's toward the end of their report the following morning, Buzz surprised everybody by taking it seriously.

"Hey! Why not?" he said. "I mean, if we put some unspiked candy in its place, how could anyone accuse us of stealing? And maybe Dino still has some more of the Belgian chocolate bars. That would make it perfect. Just imagine Vinnie's face when he sees what he thinks is—"

"That would be just stupid!" said Wacko. "Joe is absolutely right. We'd never get away with it. And it would still be a criminal offense. Breaking and entering, or something just as serious."

"But—"

"But nothing! In any case, we'd never make it past the window. It's probably wired. And even if we were stupid enough to try, when would we do it? Today—

that's when. In broad daylight. That's the only time we have left. Karen herself pointed that out. . . . Didn't she?"

Wacko had appealed to the screen. The screen replied, *"Affirmative."*

"No," said Wacko. "It would take a professional housebreaker. Someone like—uh—Kelly—that buddy of Roscoe's."

Buzz nodded. He'd been convinced for the past couple of minutes. Then he turned.

"Speaking of Roscoe, did you guys see anything of him last night?"

"No, thank goodness!" came the reply. *"But forget him, for the present. In less than nine hours, those kids will be biting into those chocolate bars if we don't do something about it. Something effective . . . Any ideas?"*

Wacko frowned.

"Well, I've been giving it some thought. Quite a lot of thought. Like about the people who might listen and take it seriously."

"So?"

All the ghosts were very alert. They themselves had been thinking hard, too—but without any really positive results.

"Well, first, of course, there's the senator himself."

The screen flickered.

"Aw, come on, Wacko! We—"

The message ended abruptly. Joe had told Carlos to let his old friend finish. Wacko wasn't the sort to come up with anything wild and foolish.

"Sorry, Wacko! Go on."

"And of course," said Wacko, giving the space in

front of the word processor a sour look, "as we all know, the senator won't be arriving until it's too late." He paused. "So next," he continued, "there's the senator's staff. Well, that's pretty useless, too. The senior members are all with him, probably on the plane by now. So we can't get word to *them* in time, either."

"What about the junior members?" said Buzz.

Wacko shook his head.

"This is Saturday, remember. And even if we could get through to any of them at home, they'd only laugh or hang up, thinking it's a Halloween hoax. Even if they didn't, they'd be too scared to touch it, once we told them the name of the spiker. 'A member of the senator's family?' " Wacko rolled his eyes in mocking imitation of some timid junior secretary. " 'Wow! Forget it!' "

"So go on. What *do* you have in mind?"

"I'm getting there," said Wacko. "I just want you all to be clear about what our options are."

"He gets this from his father," said Carlos, proudly. "You can tell he's a lawyer's son when—"

"Be quiet, Carlos!" said Joe. "Let's hear what he has to say."

"—there's Josephine," Wacko was continuing. "But we've already ruled her out, too. Because even if she believed us and challenged Vinnie, he'd throw it right back and make it look like she was covering for Lester."

"Still," murmured Joe, "if it helped save those trick-or-treaters from injury . . ."

But Wacko had a better idea. Much better.

"But there *is* one person we haven't tried. Someone who also stands to suffer, along with the senator and the kids, if this thing goes through. Buzz has just reminded me of him."

"Huh?" Buzz looked puzzled for a moment. "Oh! You mean—?"

"Dino Gorusso. Yes."

Wacko was now permitting himself a faint smile.

"Of course!" said Karen. "The second bird!"

"Bird?" said Danny.

"The one Vinnie was bragging about," said Karen. "When he told Jeanine he was hoping to kill two birds with one stone."

"Hold it!" said Joe. His eyes were gleaming. He looked more thoughtful now than he'd ever looked in the past couple of days. "Tell Wacko congratulations," he said to Carlos. "Tell him I'm kicking myself for not thinking of Dino earlier. Then put them on hold. I need to work out a few details. We have to make the best possible use of this idea in the time we have left."

It didn't take Joe long to work out a strategy.

"There's only one thing you can do," the message flickered. *"That is to go to Dino and tell him everything you know about the plot—without mentioning us, of course. Dino's an old friend of the senator's, and he'll be able to claim a word with him the minute he gets home. What he'll tell the senator exactly, we don't know. But you can be sure of two things. One: He'll be able to convince the senator that this is no hoax. And two: He'll do it discreetly, so the TV people won't get wind of it."*

110

"You really think so?" said Buzz.

"He's sure to. Dino has a lot to lose, too. And he won't want any adverse publicity, either. Leave it to him. Just make sure you reach him, is all—the sooner the better. We'll be right behind you."

"We're on our—"

But a new message had started to form, even as Wacko was reaching for the OFF switch.

"Wait! One more thing. Joe says as an extra precaution—a fail-safe—a last resort—you'd better dig out something spooky to wear, when you're through seeing Dino."

"Us?" said Wacko, looking round with an uncertain grin. "Buzz and I?"

"Affirmative!"

"But why?" asked Buzz, looking just as bemused as Wacko.

"Because this evening, you two are going to that Halloween party. You're going to gate-crash it. It shouldn't be too difficult with all the fuss of the senator's homecoming, and with a TV crew creating extra confusion. Besides, you're kids yourselves really, and The Children's Senator isn't going to have you thrown out if he thinks you've made a genuine mistake."

"Yes, but—" Buzz was still baffled. *"Then what?"*

"This is 'then what.' If all else fails—if for some reason you can't get hold of Dino, or he won't cooperate after all—then you two will just have to grab that box of chocolate bars the second the senator looks ready to start dishing them out. Before anyone can start chewing on them. OK? And then you'll explain what's in them. In fact, you'll break a couple open and show what's in them."

"But Vinnie'll still be able to put the blame on Lester," said Wacko, looking very uncomfortable at the prospect of this new assignment.

"Maybe he'll have a shot at putting the blame on me and Wacko, too," said Buzz.

"And the senator would *still* be made to look bad," said Wacko.

There was a pause again. Then the screen began to flicker.

"Joe says he's sorry and he knows how you must feel. But he did say it was only as a last resort. And at least it would save those kids from any horrible physical injuries. But look. Try Dino first. He'll probably come up with something better. . . . Hey, and cheer up! At least he might be able to rent you a couple of spook suits—at discount rates!"

15
The
Clean Conspiracy

As it happened, Dino was doing a brisk trade in Halloween masks when Buzz and Wacko stepped inside his store that morning. It was a big old barn of a place, with only one small display window. In honor of the season, that window was crammed with masks of all kinds: devils, vampires, goblins, skeletons, witches, werewolves—and an especially gruesome bunch of creatures from outer space.

And *crammed* was certainly the word.

The masks looked as if they'd simply been tossed in there in random fistfuls, and when the boys looked around, just inside the door, they saw that the window recess was being used as an extra counter, with another heap of masks spilled out onto the upturned cartons and crates in which they'd originally arrived. Other upturned cartons and crates were ranged about elsewhere in the store, in regular but ragged rows and islands, and these also served as counters for the articles they'd contained. Apparently, Dino didn't believe in fancy furnishings, as a large banner high on the far wall proclaimed.

YOU WANT BEAUTIFUL DISPLAYS?
GO TO SAKS OR BLOOMIES!
YOU WANT GREAT BARGAINS?
COME TO DINO'S DISCOUNTS!

Dino himself was presiding as usual, on a raised platform area next to the checkout. He was sitting on a tall bar stool—a perch that undoubtedly gave him a greater command of the whole store. On the other hand, the stool's spindly legs made that perch seem so precarious that mothers had been known to leave their small kids at the foot of the platform while they themselves browsed around the "counters"—telling the children to watch closely and if they were good they might get to see the man fall off his stool.

And that would have been one spectacular crash, for Dino Gorusso was a very big man. He was not especially tall, but he weighed at least 250 pounds, a great deal of which was solid muscle. This muscle bulged so ominously under his tight red sweater that it didn't seem likely he'd ever need to use the baseball bat leaning against the stool—a deterrent to any would-be stickup artist who might have designs on the cash register.

"I told ya already, lady!" he was bawling across to someone in the cluster of people rummaging among the masks. "You buy two, ya get one free. And at those prices, it's a steal anyway!"

As he spoke, his eyes were flitting about in the shadow of the visor of the Giants cap he was wearing.

"You find someplace that'll sell y'a toaster at a bigger discount than that, mister," he called to someone else, at the other end of the store, "and I'll give you a year's supply of Italian bread to go with it. For free."

Then his eyes lit on Buzz and Wacko, just beneath him, and his round, pleasant face became distorted with mock anger. "OK, you two! If you don't wanna buy them, take those ugly masks off and put 'em back on the pile where you got them from!" Then he grinned. "What can I do for you?"

"At least he has a sense of humor," Karen murmured.

"Yeah!" grunted Danny. "But let's hope he still has it when they tell him what they want!"

"He won't be laughing, that's for sure!" said Carlos.

"Be quiet, you three, and listen," said Joe.

Wacko was doing the talking.

"It's—uh—sort of confidential," he said, glancing around at the nearby check-out girl and the other people drifting about in that corner of the store.

"You want credit, the answer's no already," said Dino, firmly.

"No, sir," said Buzz. "It's—we—it's about some chocolate bars. Belgian."

Dino's eyes had narrowed to slits, whether in suspicion or puzzlement it was hard to tell.

"So?"

Wacko took a deep breath. Then, keeping his voice low, he leaned forward and said: "It's also about Senator Boyars. He's in trouble—only he doesn't know it. And we need your help."

Dino's eyes flashed. He too lowered his voice as, with remarkable nimbleness for one so heavy, he got down from his perch.

"I don't know what you're tryin'a tell me, but this better be on the level."

"It is, sir," said Wacko. "It really is. And it's urgent."

"OK, come with me," said Dino. "Marie—you keep an eye on the store. And don't let any these deadbeats talk you into making extra discounts or we don't eat at *all*, next week!"

"That'll be the day!" murmured the check-out girl, smiling, as Dino led the two boys to the back of the store.

There was a battered old door there. It looked as if it might lead to a scene of even greater messiness— until Dino held it open for them.

Buzz's eyes widened. The room they were entering was more like something he'd have expected to find in a luxury office building. There was a thick green wall-to-wall carpet; a large light oak desk on elegant steel legs; several small but comfortable-looking easy chairs; a yucca plant; and a big, high-backed, black leather swivel chair behind the desk.

"Come on, hurry it up!" Dino said to Wacko, who'd been lagging behind in order to make sure their four companions would have time to enter, too. "Customers see how nice I got it in here, they'll get ideas that maybe my prices aren't low *enough*. Those jerks, they got only one aim in life—to put Dino Gorusso in the poorhouse."

Once inside the office with the door shut, however, Dino became a different man—quieter, more serious, yet somehow, despite that, younger looking.

"Take a seat," he told them, moving behind the desk and sitting in the black chair. He took off the cap and smoothed back his short, black, slightly curling hair. He placed the cap directly in front of him on the desk, the visor pointing toward the boys, then clasped his huge hands and rested them on the edge of the desk. This seemed to give the cap a strange significance, as if it were a crystal ball or—more appropriately, as it turned out—some kind of lie-detecting apparatus.

"OK," he said. "Now tell me what all this is about. . . . But first," he went on, giving Wacko a very sharp look, "tell me this. You. Don't I know you?"

Wacko gulped.

"I—I don't know, sir. I once bought some computer parts here, but—"

"Ah, yeah!" Dino's face had cleared. "You and that kid, the one that got burned." He frowned slightly. "I was sorry to hear about that."

"I could *tell* he was a nice guy!" said Carlos, turning to the others. "He remembers me!"

"Yes," Wacko was replying. "Carlos Gomez. But it wasn't any fault in the components you sold us. It—"

"*I* know that!" snapped Dino. "Nobody has to tell me *that!* I just don't handle substandard products. I handle bankruptcy inventories, surplus supplies, end-of-line products. That's how *I* keep my prices down. And I don't handle any stolen goods, either!" he added fiercely. "No matter what some creeps might say behind my back!"

"No, sir," said Buzz. "We—"

But Dino interrupted. His flare-up had died down some, but he was still staring thoughtfully—and rather suspiciously—at Wacko.

"Isn't your father a lawyer in the state's attorney's office?"

"Yes, but this has nothing to do with him."

Dino didn't seem to hear. He was gazing down at his clasped hands, or the cap, or some space between.

"I mean, this stuff about Senator Boyars." He raised his eyes and flashed the two visitors a challenging glance. "Who is one real helluva fine guy!" Then he lowered his eyes and continued quietly. "This stuff about the senator and the Belgian candy you mentioned. It isn't anything political, is it? I mean, no one up at the capital is trying to smear him, saying he's cheap for handing out discount candy, huh? Because"—he looked up and fixed Wacko with a steady burning stare—"lemme tell you this. I'll deny absolutely that I ever did sell him anything like that!"

He sat back then, and swiveled slightly from side to side, giving Buzz the same stare.

Buzz shook his head.

"The only one who's trying to smear the senator," he said, "is his stepson, Vinnie. Why don't you let us tell you what we've found out? Then you can judge for yourself."

At the mention of Vinnie, the lightly clasped hands

tightened noticeably. Otherwise, as far as the two boys were concerned, Dino seemed to relax his guard.

"Yeah," he murmured. "Sure. . . . Sorry! . . . Go right ahead."

Dino's expression went through several phases as the boys recounted what they had found out about the plot. At the first mention of Vinnie's name, that expression had already darkened. But when they told him of Vinnie's occupation with the needles and the chocolate bars, it went positively black. This blackness of anger then gave way to a look of sheer contempt when Jeanine and her cowardly complicity were mentioned, and that in turn was squeezed out by a silent snarl of disgust when they told him of Vinnie's plans to incriminate Lester if need be, and of the steps he'd already taken to cover this.

"The jerk!" he muttered. "That's just what he *would* do!"

"You know him?" said Wacko. "I mean, well enough to—?"

"Sure I know him! He tried for credit once—and I let him have it on account of him being the senator's stepson. I let him have a stereo, and he never paid a cent, and the next thing I know, he's sold it someplace else and used the cash for gambling. Then he comes asking for a video recorder, also credit, and this time I tell him to get lost. That's when he got real nasty. . . . *Sure* I know him! What you been telling me doesn't surprise me one little bit. I only wish I'd done what I told him I'd do then, if he didn't get outa my store, fast."

119

"What was that, sir?" Buzz asked quietly, as Dino glowered at his cap.

"Stick my thumb in his eye!" murmured Dino, without looking up. Then he sighed. "But you have to hand it to him, I guess. The rat is real clever. He's really got it all sewed up by the sound of it."

"We were hoping—"

But Dino was still talking, frowning, not so much angry now as worried.

"I mean, for me, I ain't all that bothered. But the senator—even if you do gate-crash the party and make sure everyone sees how dangerous those chocolate bars are—the senator's gonna be badly hurt. And that's too bad!"

He got up and stood by the black chair.

"You see this?" he said, giving it a spin. "*He* bought me this. When I first started this business. It was a promise he'd made years before. Just after my last brush with the law. I was just eighteen. *I'd* been an orphanage kid, too, like those kids tonight, and he'd been taking an interest in me, and I guess I'd let him down. But he was in court that day, and he spoke up on my behalf. Anyway, after the judge had given me a suspended sentence, I was still feeling kinda perky, so when the senator says to me, 'I hope you'll leave here today with some really worthwhile aim for the future, Dino,' I played it kinda cool. 'Sure, senator,' I said. 'I been looking at that judge's chair all day, and that's gonna be my aim.' 'Oh?' he says. 'Sure!' I said. 'I aim to get me one just like it, soon as I have enough money.' "

He glanced at the two boys as he sat down again.

"Nargh! Don't smile. It wasn't funny. Just smartass talk. But underneath, I really had learned my lesson, you understand? And I really was grateful to the senator. And—well—when I did make good, this was waiting for me, all nicely gift-wrapped." He took a deep breath. "Which is why I'll do anything to help that guy. Anything. If—if I can."

He studied his cap again, as if it might yield up some bright idea.

"By the way," he said, after a few moments, "who told you about this—all these details?"

"Uh-oh!" said Karen. "Here we go again!"

But she needn't have worried. The question that had proved such a stumbling block in Detective Grogan's office was a mere pebble in Dino's.

"Some friends," said Buzz. "They were—uh—doing a job in the senator's backyard, and they overheard Vinnie telling his girlfriend."

"In fact, they actually saw him sticking the needles in," said Wacko. "It wasn't something Vinnie was just saying."

"What kind of job? You mean something legit? Like leaf raking?"

"Yes. Sort of. They—they just don't want anyone to know they were—well—eavesdropping."

Dino smiled briefly.

"And they want to keep their names outa this, huh? I know *that* tune!" Then he looked worried again. "Not that it matters. The problem is, how do we stop this? Without exposing the senator's white lie?"

"And without getting Lester framed," Buzz put in.

"Yeah, yeah. . . ." Dino was thinking hard now, studying every stitch in the Giants cap.

"All *we* could think of," said Buzz, "was breaking

into the senator's den sometime between now and party time and substituting a box of unspiked candy for the one with the needles in."

"All *he* could think of was that," said Wacko. "I think it's a dumb idea, and so do—"

Just in time, Wacko checked himself from saying, "and so do the others." Instead, he began to outline Joe's idea, that maybe Dino could say something to the senator at the last minute—something that would cover all the bases: protecting the trick-or-treaters, the senator's reputation and Lester's innocence. Even as he did this, Wacko had a sinking feeling, realizing how feeble the plan sounded, how over-optimistic.

But Dino wasn't even listening. He'd just had a better idea. A *much* better idea. A big boyish smile was lighting up his face.

"Hey! Yeah!" he said, interrupting Wacko. "I mean, sure—it *would* be a dumb move—for *you* to break in and make the switch. But an expert—I mean a real pro—or a real ex-pro—wow! And I know just the fella for the job!"

"You do, sir?"

Both boys were staring at him.

"Yeah! The Ghost!"

They nearly leaped out of their chairs at that.

"The—what?" gasped Buzz, looking over his shoulder uneasily—not realizing that Danny, just behind him, was going through the same reaction, having been standing right in the spot that Dino seemed to have been staring at.

"Yeah!" said Dino, grinning, and getting up so fast it set his chair rocking wildly. "That was his old professional name. Shelley the Ghost. On account of he was so good."

"Uh—how?" asked Wacko as Dino made his way to a second door, in the wall behind them.

Dino paused, with his hand on the doorknob.

"He was the best in the business. Breaking and entering. Never left a trace, ever. No one ever saw him coming, no one ever saw him leave. Even on a daylight job. And since it'll be getting dark today around 5:15, 5:30—it should be a breeze."

"Do you think he'd do it, sir?" asked Buzz, his fingers tightly crossed.

"You bet he will! He's legit now. In fact, he works for me, back here, in the storeroom. But the senator once helped him, too, and Shelley's like me—he never forgets that kinda support." Dino opened the door. "Hey! Shelley!" he called out, into a cavern that seemed to be stacked from floor to ceiling with crates. "You want to come in here a minute? I got a special job you might be interested in."

Dino walked back to his desk, sat down and grinned.

"You come to Dino with a problem. It's about a dirty conspiracy, right? Well, maybe you'll get lucky. Maybe Dino can fix it so you can trade in that dirty conspiracy for a nice *clean* conspiracy. . . . Hi, Shelley! I want you to listen to what these two kids have got to tell you."

The boys turned sharply.

The little man who had to be Shelley—Shelley the Ghost—had slipped in so quietly and unobtrusively they hadn't even noticed.

Even the four real ghosts had been taken by surprise.

16
The Visit of Count Dracula, the Undead—and Shelley the Ghost...

"It's over on the far left. Not the very end corner room—that's the library. But the next one to it, around the corner, on the side of the building."

The time was 5:20. The afterglow was just beginning to fade from the sky above the Boyars residence. Buzz and Wacko, each with a bundle of cloth under his arm, were pointing up at the house, while the man with them kept glancing in that direction, then back at the large box-shaped parcel he was holding.

The man was . . .

But it was mainly what he *wasn't* that were his strong features.

He wasn't tall, yet he wasn't short. He certainly wasn't fat, but he wasn't particularly thin, either. His hair was a dusty brown—or was it rusty gray? He *might* have been clean-shaved; then again, he might have been wearing a small mustache, cut so short that it was no more than a strip of extra-long stubble.

His age could have been anything between twenty-five and sixty-five. Or even twenty to sixty. Or possibly thirty to seventy . . . Even his clothes would have been difficult to describe. He wore a sort-of-kind-of fatigues-top tunic with matching pants. It vaguely suggested a deliveryman's uniform—though this may have been an illusion created by the parcel and the dubious, deliveryman-like way he kept glancing at it, as the boys gave their directions. The uniform, if it was a uniform, was neither mailman-blue nor UPS-brown, but something as dusty and indeterminate as the rest of him.

Dusty and indeterminate. No stranger ever gave Shelley the Ghost a second glance. Even trained police officers detailed to keep watch on him had been known to lose track of him after a couple of blocks. This was because Shelley-on-the-move was even harder to focus on than Shelley-stationary. He simply seemed to fade into the background by day and merge with the shadows by night.

Just then, as dusk began to fall and he moved along the road, away from the gates but keeping close to the fence that bounded the Boyars property, Shelley did both—fading and merging, merging and fading, until, after what couldn't have been more than about twenty unhurried (yet not exactly slow) paces, he'd disappeared.

"Where'd he go?" gasped Buzz, blinking.

"I'm not sure," said Wacko. "But—hey—let's not just stand here gaping. We have to be up there, creating our diversion, within the next five minutes."

Having said that, Wacko took out a set of vampire

teeth and fixed them in his mouth, over his own. Then he unrolled the dark cloth bundle, which turned out to be a cape, and put it over his shoulders.

"Meetch Countch Dracula!" he said, struggling to get control over the teeth.

Buzz glanced around, blushing slightly. He was glad the senator lived on a quiet back road, on the outskirts of town.

"Masks would have been simpler!" he grunted, unfurling his bundle and slipping on a white hooded bathrobe. Then he took out a pair of bug-eyed glasses, to which a long, greenish, wart-encrusted nose was attached, and put them on. "What did Dino say *this* novelty was called?"

"The Face of the Undead!" said Wacko, grinning, proud to have managed the word *Face* without sloshing again. "Come on, Buzz. *You* know why masks wouldn't have been any good. How could the others get in touch with us if our ears and lips were covered?"

As if in answer, both boys felt a series of faint cool flicks on their right earlobes.

"Correct!" the message seemed to say. Or, more probably: "Correct! But now get a move on, or Shelley will be there before you!"

There were lights in many of the senator's windows tonight. They seemed to gather strength in the increasing darkness, even as the two uneasily garbed figures hurried up the driveway. But the brightest lights of all were behind the portico, near the main door—brilliant, glaring lights that kept shifting around.

126

"That'll be the TV people," said Wacko. "Getting set up."

"Yeah," said Buzz. "That looks like their van at the side, over on the right. Glad it's not over on the left. Even Shelley might have found it tough if it had been there."

Wacko nodded. Dark figures could be seen bustling about between the main door and the van.

"Looks to me like there's diversion enough, without us," he said, as they approached the terrace. "There's more of them in the hallway, too. Including Vinnie and Lester. I bet everyone in the house is over at this side, watching."

"Let's hope so, anyway . . . How do I look?"

"Horrible!"

"Good! That makes two of us. Hey, watch out for these cables!"

The terrace looked as if all the hibernating snakes in the neighborhood had wakened up and decided to come trick-or-treating. As Buzz stumbled over one of them, someone called out, "These'll have to be tidied up before the senator arrives. We don't want the old boy falling flat on his face."

"Don't worry, Mike," said another man, standing at the open door. "They will be." Then he turned to the boys. "Hey! Who are you? You're early, aren't you?"

He was a tall man, bald, wearing a silvery windbreaker and carrying a clipboard.

"We—we've come for the party," said Buzz, blushing again behind the encrusted nose, feeling rather foolish all of a sudden.

The man glanced at the clipboard, flipping over a few pages.

"I thought this was just for the orphanage kids? Arriving 6:45 to 7:00? In a bunch?"

Buzz looked at Wacko. Wacko coughed nervously.

"Uh—trick or treat!" was all he managed to come up with, in a very feeble un-Dracula-like voice.

"You'd better wait there," said the man. He turned and called back into the house. "Hey, Mr. Boyars! Is it OK to let these kids in?"

Vinnie came forward. He had dressed himself carefully for the occasion, with a shirt and tie and a gray suede jacket. He smirked at the TV man, then scowled at the newcomers.

"Who invited you?" he said.

"We heard there was—uh—going to be a party," mumbled Buzz.

"They're just a couple of gate-crashers," said a young woman, pushing forward, holding a golden retriever by the collar.

The dog's was the only friendly face around, it seemed to Buzz just then.

"We're not, miss!" he said. "He"—he gave Wacko an impatient nudge—"he's Lester's cousin."

"Uh—yeah!" said Wacko. "I'm Lesht—uh—Lester's cousin."

Vinnie's dimple deepened.

"Is that so?" he drawled. "Then Josephine must have invited you, right?" Before Wacko could answer, Vinnie turned and bawled over his shoulder: "Hey, Josephine! Who gave you permission to invite *all* your grandchildren?"

Josephine came forward and peered at Wacko. Wacko removed his fangs, much as he might have tipped his cap.

"Oh, it's *you!*" said Josephine. Then she looked up at Vinnie. "He isn't no grandchild of mine, Mr. Vinnie, and that's the truth."

"Yeah, gramma, but he *is* my cousin!"

Now it was Lester's turn to push forward.

"Hi, Henry!" he said.

"Hi, Lester!" said Wacko. He replaced the fangs, and Lester laughed and clapped his hands. Wacko turned to Vinnie. "You can be cousins without sharing the same grandmother, you know."

It sounded cold, even through the fangs. Vinnie took a step forward.

"Don't get fresh with *me*, sonny, or I'll shove those fangs down your throat! Now—"

"Hey!" shouted one of the men outside. "D'you mind holding your debate someplace else? We're trying to get the lights fixed."

"In fact," said the bald man, placing a friendly hand on Vinnie's shoulder, "why don't we put them to work, Mr. Boyars? We could use them as stand-ins to try out the lighting. That black cape, that white robe. Half the kids who're coming will be dressed like that, and we *must* get the balance right."

Vinnie was smirking again. The TV man had obviously gotten his measure. The friendly hand and the respectful tone had done their job.

"Sure! Why not?" Then the smirk became a snigger as he nudged Jeanine. "The more the merrier, after all!"

Meanwhile, the four real ghosts were watching Shelley at work.

Seemingly from the depths of a large flower tub, he had suddenly appeared, just when some of them were beginning to wonder if he'd lost his way—and now he was examining the den window. It was fairly dark along that side of the building by contrast with the blaze of lights at the front, but here too Shelley was exhibiting certain ghostlike qualities. Not for him a shaded flashlight at this stage, out in the open. Instead, he seemed to be gifted with the keener night vision of the true ghost as he stood there, as casually relaxed as if he'd been the handyman of the house, sent there to examine a crack in one of the panes of glass—which he was doing mainly with his fingers, lightly running them around the edges of the panes. At his feet, the large boxlike parcel once again helped to create the right illusion. It looked for all the world like the handyman's portable tool chest.

"I hope he's able to get in there without raising the alarm," said Karen.

"He knows what he's doing," said Carlos. "You can tell that just by looking at him."

"Even if he did trigger the alarm, they might never hear it, around there," said Joe, with a grin.

The argument at the door was reaching its climax. One of the men was yelling for the arguers to get out of the way.

Then:

"Hey! Look out!" said Danny. "There's someone over there. I think he's spotted Shelley!"

They caught a glimpse of a dark shape at the corner, silhouetted by the glow from the TV lamps. Then the shape turned abruptly and went back around the front, out of sight.

But there was no hue and cry.

They listened, peering in that direction, for several seconds.

"Probably one of the TV crew," said Joe. "Probably wondering if it might be better with an extra light at this end. I don't think he even noticed Shelley."

"I wish Shelley would hurry up, though," said Karen. "He's—"

Then she blinked.

Shelley wasn't there anymore. In the few seconds they'd been diverted by the man at the corner, Dino's friend had disappeared.

There was only a slight opening at the bottom of the window—which had previously been shut—to show that he'd been there at all.

"He's in already!" gasped Carlos, pointing to a faint glow at the bottom of the drapes—a glow that hadn't been there before.

"I'm glad to see he needs a flashlight *sometimes*," murmured Karen. "I was beginning to think he was more of a ghost than us. Made me feel quite creepy!"

"Let's hope he'll be able to switch the chocolate bars OK," said Danny, still anxious.

"Are you kidding?" said Carlos. "Buzz and Wacko told him exactly where the key is. There's nothing to stop him now. Especially with that racket going on."

The barking of a dog was now augmenting the general hubbub.

"Let's see what's going on," said Joe.

Buzz and Wacko were still standing under the lights outside the main door. A short, stocky man with glasses was with them. He was holding a hand microphone. He turned to the open door as the ghosts approached. "Hey!" he yelled. "For Pete's sake! Get that dog out of there!"

As the four looked through into the hall, they saw that it was Dana who was making the racket. But it certainly wasn't Dracula or the Undead who'd spooked her. Her bristling head was turned toward the staircase, at the side of the hall.

Jeanine crouched beside the dog, gripping the collar.

"Hush, baby, hush!"

"Never mind the baby talk!" snapped Vinnie. "You heard what the man said. Get her out of here!"

"Come on, Dana," said Jeanine. "Let's see if Josephine has a bone for you."

As the woman was leading the dog away, through an inner door, Buzz murmured something to Wacko. Joe was close enough to hear what he said.

"I wonder if Shelley's made it inside yet?"

Before Wacko could reply, Joe touched them both on the right ears. The Undead's eyes brightened behind the gruesome glasses, and Dracula exposed his fangs in a broad drooling smile.

"OK, you two!" said the man with the microphone. "I want you to look up at the open door like the senator has just opened it. OK? So say 'Trick or treat!' like you mean it."

"Let's slip through while we have the chance," said Joe.

The hall was so big that the stairs—wide though

132

they were—wide and grand, with a fancy balustrade—took up only one corner. There was a fine, dark, Spanish oak sideboard along one wall, several mirrors, a grandfather's clock that was registering five minutes to six—and of course a profusion of television lights and busy people.

"No," the bald man was saying, "let's not even *try* for the clock in the background. *This* is where the senator will be standing—right here by this sideboard—giving out the candy, with the kids filing on past, through the door at the rear and into the kitchen for some real food. We want to keep it lively. This isn't a feature on antiques."

Jeanine had now returned to the hall by that same door. She took her place with Vinnie and Lester, just in front of it.

"How much time do we have, Sam?" asked the man with the microphone, looking in.

"Before the senator arrives?" The bald man glanced at his watch, then at the clipboard. "Maybe forty-five minutes, Tom. But don't count on more than thirty."

The microphone man turned back to the boys outside.

"Again!"

"Trick or treat!"

"Again! Sound like you mean it. You've just come from the orphanage. You're bubbling over with merry mischief and the senator is pretending to be scared out of his socks."

"TRICK OR TREAT!"

That's when the dog started barking again. Even from behind the closed door, it sounded very loud.

"What's with it *now?*" snarled Vinnie.

Jeanine was already going through, into the back.

"She—oh—she's down near the library, I think!"

Joe looked at the others.

"The den!" he said. "I bet the dog's outside the den! I bet she's heard Shelley!"

"Well, go see, then!" said Vinnie to Jeanine, going to the rear door and opening it wider. "And make sure she *stays* quiet this time!"

The ghosts were already on their way. Carlos had overtaken Jeanine before she'd even reached the corner of the corridor.

Sure enough, Dana was outside the den, sniffing and growling at the crack under the door.

"Divert her, Carlos!" Joe shouted. "Quick—before—"

"What's going on?"

Vinnie had decided to see for himself. In his annoyance, he was moving almost as fast as Carlos.

But the young ghost had beaten them all to it, and, prancing in front of the dog, beyond the den, had managed to get Dana to do her growling and whimpering farther along the corridor.

"It—it's just the excitement," said Jeanine, rushing to comfort her pet—and also, probably, to come between the dog and the threatening foot of the angry Vinnie.

"Well, shut her in my room, then, until it's all over! Go on!"

Carlos stopped cavorting and let Jeanine lead the dog away, without upsetting Dana any further. Vinnie went with her part of the way, still threatening what he'd do if the dog caused one more interruption.

"Wow! That was close!" said Danny.

"It could have blown everything!" said Karen.

Joe looked worried.

"Yeah! I only hope it didn't scare Shelley off before he made the switch."

They listened at the den door.

Absolute silence.

Then they heard Vinnie and Jeanine on their way back to the hall, and the ghosts had to tear themselves away, still unsure.

17
...Plus Frankenstein's Monster

From that point on, things began to get even more hectic.

When the ghosts slipped back into the hall with Jeanine and Vinnie, they found that Buzz and Wacko had been brought in for more tests.

"OK," the man with the microphone was saying. "This is where the senator will be handing out the treats. I want you to pretend I have some in my hand."

This obviously amused Vinnie. He gave Jeanine a nudge. His dimple seemed to wriggle with secret glee.

". . . and remember," the man continued, "although the kids are going to be given a bang-up meal in the kitchen, there's sure to be some kids who'll want to sample the candy right away. OK?"

"Oh, sure!" murmured Vinnie, almost squirming with pleasure. "You bet!"

"So, you two, let's see you move toward that door,

making like you're stuffing candy into your mouths."

Very self-consciously, the boys went through this charade—Wacko glancing accusingly at Vinnie as he did so.

Vinnie was in a very good mood now. Even Jeanine had cheered up some—though her smile as she watched the boys was far from pleasant.

The bald man stepped forward.

"Yes," he said. "That's good. You know, Tom, it would make quite a shot if some kid with fangs, like this one, tried chewing really sticky candy with *them* in his mouth. Kind of cute." He turned to Vinnie. "Do you know what sort of treat the senator has in mind?"

Vinnie flushed slightly.

"Well, he's supposed—uh—he's planning to be bringing it with him from Belgium. My guess is it'll be chocolate." Then he chuckled, and four ghost hands and two living ones itched to slap him across the mouth. "But I bet that'll make quite a shot, with or without fangs!"

The man called Tom shrugged.

"Maybe if none of them *is* wearing fangs, we can use this kid. Why don't we try—?" He broke off. "*Now* what?" he groaned.

Beyond the open outer door, someone had bawled, "Hey, you! Watch where you're putting those big feet!"

Then they stared as a slow ponderous figure loomed into the glare of the lights, tromping over the cables.

The feet certainly were big. The people in the hall—ghosts and living alike—stared at the huge boots as they paused on the threshold. Then their eyes traveled up—over the rough dark pants and ragged sweater—to the ghastly greenish white head.

Under those lights, it seemed at first to be all forehead—a forehead seamed with livid stitches and studded here and there with small steely bolts.

"Who on earth's this?" whispered the bald man.

Karen giggled.

"Frankenstein's Monster—who else?" she said.

But Joe's grin soon faded.

"It's the 'who else' part that bothers *me!*" he murmured.

Vinnie had gone to the door—either to greet or order off the stranger. It seemed very much like the latter until the monster, grunting in true Frankenstein fashion, pulled out a slim wallet and held it out so that the silver badge shone up into Vinnie's eyes.

"Pu-police?" said Vinnie, going almost as pale as the mask he was staring at.

"Just routine, sir," said the monster.

"Grogan!" gasped Carlos, recognizing the voice.

"Halloween detail," the detective was continuing. "We've had word that some burglary team is operating in the neighborhood, hoping to take advantage of party goings-on. It's probably a rumor," he added, and for a second the eyes behind the mask's slits gleamed in the direction of Buzz and Wacko, "but I thought I'd stop by anyway, and say hello to the senator."

"Sure!" said Vinnie. He'd fully recovered his poise by now. "Come on in, officer!" He winked at Jeanine. Then he said, for the second time that evening, "The more the merrier!"

Frankenstein's Monster clumped straight across to Count Dracula and the Undead.

"Haven't we met someplace else, recently?"

Dracula wasn't quite up to it.

"Y-yesh, shir!" he stuttered and slavered.

"Probably some old graveyard!" said the Undead, quicker to recover.

"I wonder what he's really come for?" said Karen.

Joe shrugged.

"I guess he just felt uneasy. I mean, all right—so he gives Buzz and Wacko the brush-off because they won't go by the rules and tell him who told *them* about this. But he must have decided that if there *is* any truth in the rumor, he'd better be on hand."

"Sure!" said Carlos. "It'd look real bad if anyone got hurt and he'd ignored the warning."

"He's going to be mad at Buzz and Wacko when nothing does happen!" said Karen.

Joe frowned.

"It's still *if*, remember. *If* nothing happens. We still don't know whether Shelley got scared off before he'd had time to make the switch."

"Hey—yeah!" said Carlos, looking alarmed. "But Buzz and Wacko will *think* he's made it. What if he hasn't? They won't be going into the last-resort routine and snatching the box out of the senator's hands the way we'd planned. Not now!"

Joe nodded. His face was as grim as the detective's monster mask, over on the other side of the hall.

"We'll just have to watch very carefully," he said. "And, if necessary, give them the reddest red alert they've ever felt!"

"Yes, but how will we know it's necessary?" said Danny.

"By looking carefully," said Joe. "Like I just said. For example, the bars in the replacement box don't have any torn wrappers, remember. And the top layer was still packed nice and tight, just the way it left the factory. You can always tell when something like that has been disturbed, if you know to look carefully."

"I sure hope so!" said Karen. "I—"

But everyone was going to the door. Someone outside had yelled, "Hey! He's here now! The senator's here!"

18
The Crunch

Karen had once been in a school play, a ballet-drama, about some old mythological version of the creation of the world. At first, when the curtain had risen, everything had been murky and dark, with flickers of lightning revealing a chaos of hissing, writhing serpents and groaning, indeterminate beasts. Then the great god Jupiter had arrived, and suddenly all was order and light.

She was reminded of this now, when the senator stepped up to the front door, with his retinue. As if by a miracle, cables had been cleared from underfoot and proper spaces made. The cameras, both outside and in the hall, were in place, ready for action, and so were the lights. Probably, of course, it had more to do with the TV people's expertise than anything magical in the senator's presence. No doubt the crew had known just how much time they had in which to make their preparations, and what had seemed like chaos had been merely the last-minute untidiness that they knew very well could be cleared up in seconds.

Senator Boyars, however, in the actual flesh, did have a striking, almost godlike appearance. He was tall and erect. His hair was white, but thick and vigorously wavy. His eyes were blue and clear and piercing, and the flesh on his tanned face looked surprisingly firm and unlined for a man of his age, especially after a grueling journey.

His retinue—a middle-aged woman secretary, a man who turned out to be his chief personal assistant and two younger aides—all had the rather limp, crumpled, weary look of people who'd been on the road or in the air for the past nine or ten hours. But Senator Boyars might only just have stepped out of a sauna.

"Vinnie, my boy!" he said, as his stepson came forward to greet him. "This *is* a surprise! I never expected *you* to be here."

"I wouldn't have missed it for the world, Dad!" said Vinnie, accepting with a sickly leer the hug the senator gave him.

The fact of Vinnie's presence seemed to put even more bounce into the senator. His eyes traveled around and didn't miss a single thing.

"Josephine!" he said, shaking the old lady warmly by the hand. "I hope this isn't putting too much of a burden on you? . . . Ah, good!" he went on, when Josephine told him she'd drafted in a couple of women to help in the kitchen, and that the orphanage people had promised to lend a hand, later. "And Lester! I'd swear you've grown a couple of inches in the last week. . . . Hi, Sam!" he said, turning to the bald man. "Glad to see *you're* in charge. Just let me know if you need anything. . . . And Tom! My favorite interviewer! I guess we can leave the hard questions until after the kids have arrived, right? . . . Speaking of kids, though—" He stared with genial perplexity at Buzz and Wacko. Then, when Wacko mumbled something in reply—"Cousin of Lester's, eh?" said the senator. "Well, any cousin of Lester's a cousin of mine!"

Only the figure of Frankenstein's Monster had him really puzzled. Then Vinnie explained, and the senator threw back his head and laughed. "Detective Eugene Grogan, of *course!*" he said, pumping the unexpected guest's hand. "I've been hearing some good things about you, up at the capital. For a minute there, in that mask, I thought you were my opponent in the last election. He had the same look about him. Especially after the votes were counted. Ha, ha, ha!"

The members of the TV crew and the retinue smiled or laughed, some wearily, some heartily. The bald man made a note on his clipboard and winked at the interviewer. The latter looked less relaxed as he glanced at his watch.

But the senator had as good a sense of timing as any of them.

"By the way," he said, after giving Jeanine a cool but pleasant smile and asking after the dog, "we picked up a monster of our own, down by the gates. Thumbing a ride, if you please!" He turned to the door. "You can come in now, Your Majesty!"

Then there was a gasp all round as in shambled the

huge, hairy figure of a gorilla. It showed its teeth in a chattering snarl and began prancing up and down.

"Meet King Kong!" said the senator. "A very dear friend of mine," he added, clapping it on the shoulder.

"Pleased to meetcha, folks!" said the gorilla—in the unmistakable tones of Dino Gorusso.

The bald man coughed politely. "Senator," he said, "the time is running on, and according to my schedule the kids should be arriving very soon. Do you have the treats ready for them?"

"Oh, sure!" said the senator, without even faltering. He pointed to a large tote bag that one of the younger men was carrying. "Lester, show Frank here to my den. Just leave the bag there, Frank, and I'll get the treats out myself in a couple of minutes. . . ." He turned to the bald man. "Well, Sam, I guess you're itching to get shots of the young monsters and witches. . . ."

The ghosts looked at one another. The senator hadn't actually told a lie, but—

"It's what you might call a politician's substitute for the truth," said Joe. "I mean, he didn't actually *say* the candy was in the bag."

"The truth's the truth," said Karen, feeling a slight pang of disappointment with her new Jupiter.

"Vinnie's enjoying it, though," said Danny. "Just look at the rat!"

Vinnie was grinning and nudging Jeanine again.

"That's because if everything went according to *his* plan, it would be just another nail in the senator's coffin," said Carlos. "When it came out that the candy was here in the house all the time."

"It looks like the senator hasn't even let his staff in on the secret," said Joe, when, as soon as Frank and Lester returned, the senator excused himself and hurried off on his own.

"I'll be right back," he said. "I'll go get the treats, and then we'll be all set."

He was only just in time. He was placing the box between two large brass candlesticks on the sideboard—the gold wrapping gleaming magically under the high-powered lights—when someone outside yelled a warning through the door.

"The bus is here now, Sam. Coming up the driveway."

The TV people had laid their plans well.

The young visitors were corralled in a bunch, out on the terrace, the lights blazing down on witches' hats, monsters' masks, capes, flapping sheets and plastic pointed ears. The cameras were busy now, of course, and so was the interviewer.

A few of the kids had been selected to come forward. The people in the hall watched and listened at the windows, which had been left half-open for that purpose.

"So you've come here trick-or-treating?" Tom said to a young witch with braces and a green face.

"Sure! *Wheee!*"

The interviewer pretended to back off a little at the rather tame witch screech that had collapsed in a giggle.

"You know who lives here, don't you?"

"Sure! Senator Boyars. *Wheee!*"

The screech had a bit more power in it this time.

145

The interviewer turned hastily to a kid with goblin ears and yellow greasepaint on his face.

"And you, young man—"

"I ain't a young man! I'm a goblin, and I'm gonna eat you!"

"Sure, sure! But first, do *you* know who lives here?"

The goblin nodded.

"And do you know that Senator Boyars has just gotten back from a long, long journey?"

"Yeah!" said the witch. "Europe!"

"Well, don't you think he'll be too tired?"

This was addressed to the whole bunch.

"NO! NO!" they roared, screamed, shrieked or growled—according to their costumes.

"We been invited!" said the witch.

"He's brought us treats, all the way from Europe!" someone else shouted.

"You aren't worried you'll scare him half to death?" said the interviewer, once more pretending to shrink back. "I mean, looking and sounding like that—you've sure scared *me!*"

"Step aside, then!" said the witch, pointing at him with a long, green, artificial fingernail. "Or I'll put a spell on you!"

"OK, OK! But knock on the door first. Maybe he'll think it's only a neighbor, then he'll *really* get a shock!"

Tom couldn't have set it up better. The kids fell under *his* spell, all right. There was dead silence when the witch knocked on the door.

Then, when the senator himself opened it, with the lights full on him, the visitors exploded.

"TRICK OR TREAT!"

The way Senator Boyars hammed it up would have

done credit to a seasoned comedy actor. Never had anyone shown such fright. Never had anyone leaped like that, hands flung up in horror. Never had anyone shaken like that, from his head to his toes. And never had anyone's knees knocked together so rapidly and violently.

"T-t-treat!" stuttered the senator, rolling his eyes. (But it was a stutter that rang out clearly, and those eyes had a twinkle in them even as they rolled.) "C-c-come on in!"

"One at a time!" growled a man from the orphanage, quickly stepping forward. "Like you were told this afternoon."

"Now for the crunch," murmured Joe, looking tense, as the kids filed in, eager and excited, but kept in good order by the man and a couple of helpers. "I'll take a good look at the top layer, and if I see any torn wrappers or anything to indicate that this is the spiked candy, I'll let you know. Carlos, Danny—stand by Buzz and Wacko, ready to alert them immediately."

"I hope you'll be able to see clearly enough, Joe," said Karen. "The senator's hand's sort of getting in the way."

The senator was standing by the sideboard, ready to dip into the golden box. His hand was poised over the top layer. He wasn't hamming fright now; just beaming down on the kids like a beardless Santa Claus. The inside camera was switched on, but the interviewer had retired to the back of the hall. Sam had called for simple straightforward shots of the kids as they lined up for their treats and continued on through the interior door on their way to the kitchen.

But first, there was a hitch in this carefully worked-out plan of Sam's—a hitch that also made Joe's *hastily* worked-out plan totally unnecessary.

"Just one moment, sir!"

Some of the trick-or-treaters gasped, genuinely scared. They'd been so busy looking at the senator and the gleaming box that they hadn't paid any attention to the other people in the hall, behind the lights. Now they were gaping at the lumbering Frankenstein's Monster as it put a very large hand on the senator's wrist.

"Hey!" Sam yelped.

"Officer!" said the senator, for the first time looking really shocked.

"Senior monsters first!" boomed Frankenstein's ghastly creation.

That broke the spell. Some of the kids laughed. Others cheered. They obviously thought it was all part of the fun, as the monster grabbed a couple of chocolate bars at random and began clumsily peeling the wrappers and peering at the chocolate.

"He doesn't know how to eat it!" said the witch, laughing. "The dumb old monster's never seen any candy before!"

"Uh—uh—it—is—uh—*good!*" declared the monster, beginning to champ away after a few very cautious nibbles. "Mm-mm!"

"Sure they're good, dummy!" Dino Gorusso's voice rang out.

Then there were more screams of delight as King Kong shambled forward, grabbed another couple of bars and shoved them into his mouth, wrappings and all, without a moment's hesitation.

"Better than bananas!" he growled, spitting out bits of foil and munching away happily.

"Thank you, fellas," murmured the senator, with an impatient edge to his voice and an I'll-see-you-later glint in his eyes as he looked at the detective. "Now, why don't we proceed?"

But the same glint was in Grogan's eyes as he clumped over to Buzz and Wacko. In fact, *he* said it outright.

"Needles, huh?" he muttered. "Every bar that didn't have a tear in its wrapper was spiked, huh? There aren't even any bars in there *with* tears in the wrappers as far as I could see." The detective wiped his mouth with the back of his hand, smearing the mask with chocolate. For some reason, this made him look more sinister than ever, so that his next muttered words made the boys shrink back more than they might have otherwise. *"I'll see you two later!"*

The ghosts had been watching and listening with mixed feelings.

"Poor old Buzz and Wacko!" said Danny. "They must feel they can't win, no matter what."

"No, but what happened did tell them—and us—something useful," said Joe. "It proved that the boxes were switched after all, and that there was no need for any last-resort action."

"Yeah," said Carlos. "The way Dino didn't hesitate said it loud and clear. He must have seen Shelley out there after the switch and made sure everything was OK."

Karen was staring at Frankenstein's Monster with a strange glow in her eyes.

"One thing it's told *me*," she said, "is that Detective Grogan is one very brave and conscientious man, whatever else we might think! *He* couldn't have known the bars were OK. Yet he went ahead and tried them first."

"Yeah!" sighed Danny, casting a glance of grudging admiration at his old adversary. "Plus he'll also be getting bawled out by the senator."

Meanwhile, the kids were filing past, each being handed a couple of bars. And, just as the bald man had foreseen, some couldn't wait. They were ripping open the wrappers and stuffing the chocolate in their mouths even before they reached the far door.

And there *was* one with Dracula fangs, after all. Sam drew him aside and directed the cameraman to take special shots as fangs, real teeth and candy got into a terrible tangle, and melted chocolate ran down the sides of the kid's mouth, much as if he'd been a real vampire and it had been blood.

"Hey!" whispered Carlos. "Just look at Vinnie!"

The senator's stepson's eyes were bulging, as he stared at those champing jaws. His face had turned a dusky red, and the dimple had deepened into a small crater. Jeanine put out a hand, touching his arm, but he shook it off angrily. Still, he kept his eyes on those champing jaws, switching only to the jaws of the next impatient kid, and the one after that, and the one after that, until the last visitor had filed through and the cameras were switched off and the bald man had sighed with relief and said, "That went just beautifully, senator!"

This seemed to waken Vinnie from his trance. At least for a few moments—long enough to walk unsteadily across to the sideboard and stare down at the box, where there was still a layer or two of the chocolate bars left.

"We'll give those out later, my boy," said the senator, misunderstanding Vinnie's concern. "Maybe Josephine and Lester and some of the helpers will appreciate them."

Vinnie didn't seem to hear. He was still staring down at the bars.

"*He* doesn't see any torn wrappers, either," said Carlos, grinning.

Then slowly—stiffly—almost mechanically—Vinnie reached out, picked up one of the bars, turned it over carefully, still staring at it, and walked slowly back to Jeanine's side, holding out the bar to her.

"You—here—take it," he said, in a low strained voice. "Take it and eat it. Now!"

"But, Vinnie—"

"I said *now!*"

Then Buzz just couldn't resist.

"It's OK, Jeanine," he said. "Go right ahead. The boxes have been switched. There aren't any phonograph needles in *this* bunch!"

Remarkably slowly, Vinnie turned to him. His eyes were widening, widening.

"What!" he muttered, in a voice that seemed to come from a great distance. "What—*what* was that you just said?"

Buzz repeated what he'd just said to Jeanine. But this time there was no smile of triumph on his lips, and he was backing away with every word he uttered.

Vinnie's face had started to get distorted. He seemed

to have difficulty controlling his mouth. His lips hardly moved, and it was as if that distant voice—distant but clearly vibrating with fury—were coming from the depths of the dark, craterlike dimple on his chin.

"You—and *him?* So that—that's why you gate- gate- cr- *gate-crashed!"*

The words and the way they were uttered sounded menacing and strange enough to the two living boys. But it was nothing to the spectacle their four colleagues were witnessing now.

"Gosh!" cried Danny. "Look! He's—he's so mad—he—he—"

"Yeah!" murmured Joe—and even he looked awed. *"He's so mad, he's beside himself!"*

And this was literally true.

Vinnie's astral body—its face working exactly as Vinnie's was, its eyes glaring and its mouth starting to froth at the corners—was slowly emerging, to stand shoulder to heaving shoulder with the enraged conspirator.

19
Vin-Ros, Inc.

Although no one but the ghosts could see what was happening, everyone else soon began to realize that there was something seriously wrong. The TV technicians broke off their clearing-up activities and stared at the stepson of their host. The senator himself stopped in mid-conversation with Sam and Tom, the genial smile frozen on his lips. Jeanine had turned very pale.

For about half a minute, Vinnie remained like that, mouthing silently and glaring at Buzz and Wacko, with the two boys standing absolutely still, not knowing what was going on, but instinctively not daring to move a muscle or say a single word.

"My boy! Are you feeling all right?"

The senator's voice caused Vinnie to twitch convulsively. The hatred that raged behind those eyes intensified. And, like a mirror image, his astral body twitched, too, and its eyes flashed.

Then Karen screamed.

Vinnie still hadn't made any movement toward the boys, which is what she and the other ghosts had been expecting. It hadn't been that, that caused the scream. It had been another movement entirely—a movement so swift that it was like the fall of a meteor.

Except that this meteor was dark—a dark blur that entered the ghosts' field of vision from somewhere above, as they stared at the phantom that had been projected out of Vinnie's physical body by the sheer force of his pent-up, baffled fury.

"Roscoe!" Danny gasped, as the swooping figure fell upon this glaring duplicate of Vinnie.

It occurred to Joe then that the Malev must have been watching them all the time. It must have been *Roscoe's* dark shape they'd seen at the corner, outside, when they'd been watching Shelley. And the first time Dana had barked, it must have been at Roscoe, when he'd entered the hall before them. Then he must have slunk up the stairs out of sight—out of the sight of other ghosts, anyway—and lurked there in the shadows, waiting for some chance to act. Because that had been where he'd leaped from. Up there.

All this flashed through Joe's mind as Vinnie's double collapsed under the weight of Roscoe—collapsed, made a feeble attempt to fight off the attacker, and suddenly, with the Malev's fingers around his throat, made one last desperate heave, collapsed again and disappeared.

"Oh, heavens! He's killed—"

Karen was going to say "Vinnie." But Vinnie still

stood there—the only signs of extra shock being that he'd closed his eyes and was swaying slightly.

"Maybe Roscoe only knocked Vinnie's ghost out," said Carlos, in a whisper. "The way Joe knocked *him* out. Right, Joe?"

But Joe wasn't listening. He was watching Roscoe closely. The Malev returned his stare, and a slow evil smile began to spread across his face. Then, as Joe braced himself—expecting another attack, this time on himself—the Malev vanished for the second time.

He'd been standing quite close to Vinnie, as close as Vinnie's double had been before Roscoe had felled it.

The four ghosts stared, bewildered. Even Joe couldn't figure out what had happened, in that split second.

Then Vinnie opened his eyes. Wide.

"Where's he gone?" said Danny, blinking. "Where's Roscoe? What happened?"

"I'm not sure," Joe said slowly. "But—oh, *no!*"

Vinnie was slowly advancing on Buzz. There was murder in his eyes now. Not the white-hot rage of a few moments ago, but cold, clear murder.

And he was walking with that peculiar catlike gait they'd seen so many times before in Roscoe himself.

"He's taken the place of Vinnie's astral body!" Joe said, in a low strained voice. "He's—he's taken possession!"

Karen shuddered. This was like a nightmare come true. This was the merging of the two monsters she'd spoken about earlier. The living and the dead. Vin-Ros, Incorporated!

As Vin-Ros slowly advanced on Buzz, he/they began to speak.

"So *you* switched the candy I'd spiked! *You* spoiled my plans to make this old fool look the cheap phony he really is!"

So far, the movements had been calm, deliberate, and the speech had been almost conversational. Others in the room heard it clearly enough, but no one as yet made any attempt to come between the advancing figure and the retreating boys. None of the living knew the extent of the danger, of course. Even when Vin-Ros paused in that ominous advance and picked up one of the heavy brass candlesticks from the sideboard, the movement was so casual and the glance he/they gave it was so calm—the glance a connoisseur might have given it if he'd spotted some mildly interesting configuration in the decoration—even *then* no one moved to intervene.

"Yes." The voice underwent a change, very slight but very chilling to the watching, knowing ghosts. "And *you*—you and *him*—the one with the fangs— you're the guys who snitched to the cops about the Hyman job. And—got—me—*killed!*"

With a sudden scream on the word *killed*, Vin-Ros launched itself at Buzz, the candlestick raised high, like a club. . . .

Joe had been feeling terrible. Too late, he realized he'd seriously underestimated Roscoe's intelligence. Whether Roscoe had been talking to some more experienced Malev in the meantime, or had figured it out for himself, or simply had had a flash of inspiration—he'd hit on the possession method of attacking the living. And Joe—the leader, the expert—had gone and lulled Buzz and Wacko into a false sense of security by telling them they didn't need to worry about *that* possibility for weeks!

He groaned. There was nothing he could do to stop Roscoe this time. Not when Roscoe was protected from other ghosts by a living body, using it like a suit of armor, or a tank.

But, even as the candlestick/club made its first vicious downward swing and Buzz sidestepped it at the last possible fraction of a second, and staggered, and slipped, and fell in a position that made any further fast evasive action impossible—even as the club was raised again, and the evil, gloating sneer came back to that shared face—the tide turned, and Roscoe lost his advantage.

Others—the living—were able to hear his words now. And those words had at last alerted some of the bystanders to the very real danger that Buzz and Wacko were in—despite the fact that none of them dreamed of the true source.

"Just hold it right there!"

The candlestick gleamed, frozen in mid-swing.

The attacker turned.

Grogan had spoken with crisp, professional authority. But it couldn't have been that alone that checked such a furious onslaught. Probably Roscoe had recognized the voice, even before Grogan had started to peel off his Monster mask.

"*You!*" screeched Roscoe, from behind *his* mask—that mask of living flesh.

It was like a rerun of yesterday's murderous attack

on the man who had shot him. But this time, of course, Roscoe had the use of another living body.

He propelled this body at Grogan now, the candlestick flailing. And for all his police training, the detective might have gone down under that attack—so furious and reckless was the power behind it—if Dino, still in his gorilla suit, and two of the TV crew hadn't weighed in.

Vin-Ros fought like a tiger, like a pair of tigers, but, as Dino sat on the arm that wielded the candlestick, and Grogan on the other arm, and the TV men on the legs, Vinnie suddenly went limp. His face was a bluish white. The foam oozed thickly around his lips. One small bubble had slid into the dimple, where it gleamed, iridescent, for a few moments. Then even that burst and was no more.

"It's a fit," said Grogan. "Call an ambulance. And the rest of you stand back."

"Is—is he—?" faltered the senator.

"He'll be OK," said Grogan. "So long as the medics get here soon."

Jeanine had fallen on her knees, sobbing, in a corner. No one paid her any attention. All eyes were on the body spread-eagled on the floor, its chest heaving with slow, softly barking rasps.

All eyes, that is, except for those of the four ghosts.

Their eyes, wide with horror, were focused on something a few feet to the side of the unconscious conspirator.

They were staring at the dark figure that had emerged from Vinnie's body. And it was dark this time not because of its clothing or any shadows. It was dark from the soles of its feet to the top of its normally blond head, dark as a stick of greenwood that has flared briefly, then smoldered and died, leaving a charred gray replica of itself, scored with a network of fissures.

This process hadn't happened slowly with Roscoe, however. It must have happened in one final flash, while he was still inside the living body, fighting like a demon against the finally overwhelming odds.

"He—burnt himself out!" whispered Danny.

Joe nodded. He heaved a great sigh.

"He was just too raw a rookie. He threw too much into that last move."

"Thank God!" said Karen.

"And—*now* look!" said Carlos.

But there was no need for his prompting.

The others were staring too, as the charred remains of Roscoe's ghostly body suddenly collapsed in a heap of what looked like ashes, and the heap dwindled, and faded, until, in the space of about thirty seconds, nothing remained.

Outside, in the distance, the siren of an ambulance could be heard, getting nearer.

Closer than that—from the kitchen—came a babble of happy voices, kids' voices.

For them, at least, it had been a great Halloween party, enlivened by some very jolly phony monsters.

"If only they knew!" murmured Karen, shivering slightly.

20
The Enigma Remains

Several things became clear in the next few days. And several things remained an enigma, as always. . . .

The truth about the Halloween Conspiracy itself was soon revealed to both the senator and Detective Grogan. Aside from the damning fragment spit out by Vinnie in that last mad attack on Buzz, Dino soon clinched matters by showing the senator, privately, the chocolate bars that Vinnie had spiked. This was of course convincing enough even without Jeanine's confession, which she made to the senator that night, the tears running down her cheeks, when it was believed that Vinnie might die.

"She doesn't seem all that bad a person, after all," Wacko said, at the next full meeting of the Ghost Squad. "At least she didn't desert her boyfriend."

"Correct!" flashed the word processor. *"And some of the things she's been able to tell the doctors—about Vinnie's behavior in the past—are proving very useful."*

The ghosts had been busy, observing developments both at the hospital and the senator's house. They'd learned, for instance, that Vinnie was likely to pull out of the coma, after all.

"His astral body has now returned. That's clear enough. But he's still very, very confused. Anyway, now that the senator's alert to how sick Vinnie has been, he's sparing no expense. It looks like Vinnie is in for a long, long course of treatment."

"Good!" said Wacko. "Maybe *he'll* be a better person, too, at the end of it."

Buzz was still frowning.

"What would have happened if Roscoe *had* killed Vinnie's astral body, though?" (He was especially anxious to get an answer to this one. He was thinking of the time when Danny had seen his—Buzz's—astral body taking an innocent sleepwalking stroll.) "Would—would Vinnie have gone on living?"

There was a pause. Carlos had had to get Joe's opinion here. Then:

"Probably. Yes. But in a deep coma. He'd have been a vegetable. Or even worse. Just an empty shell."

Wacko cleared his throat, giving his friend an uneasy, nervous glance. When he spoke, he tried to sound a less scary note.

"How about the senator? How is he taking all this? I mean knowing what he does now?"

"He's one very shook-up man. He's confided in Josephine—"

"Josephine?"

"*Yes. For all his talented and expert staff, she's the one he really seems to trust. He told her that he realizes now where he went wrong. How he'd been too deeply immersed in politics and other people's welfare to spare time for Vinnie, even when Vinnie was a school-kid, even after Vinnie's mother died. And how—these are his words—'I've been too ready to trifle with the truth, Josephine.' *"

"You're breaking my heart!" muttered Buzz, still seeing in his mind's eye that murderous, brassy, downswinging arc of the candlestick.

"Go on," said Wacko, to the space in front of the word processor.

"*Yes, well, we're only reporting what we observed. . . . So the senator then went on to say that he realizes how even his white lies must have gotten under Vinnie's skin. How he must have sounded like a terrible hypocrite to Vinnie—a guy the senator was always criticizing for telling lies.*"

Buzz was still not ready to listen to any excuses for Vinnie's behavior. He changed the subject.

"How about Grogan?" he asked. "Is he going to charge Vinnie with anything?"

"*No. You'd have heard from him by now if he was. He did say something at first about how he might have to book Vinnie for attacking you and making threats. Also assaulting a police officer. But he soon stopped that when he heard what the doctors had to say. Plus, of course, what the senator had to say. The senator doesn't want the matter to go any further, as you can understand.*"

"No," said Wacko. "I bet he doesn't!"

"And how about Roscoe?" said Buzz. "Do you really think that was the last of him?"

Again, there was a pause. Then:

"*On this earth, in this phase of ghosthood, yes. But who knows? The ghost of his ghost has probably gone on to another level. There could be many levels yet. For all of us.*"

Wacko nodded. He was looking anxious, strained.

"Do you—do you think he *did* speak to some other Malev?" he asked. "Between being knocked out and showing up at the senator's place?"

"Yeah!" said Buzz, suddenly startled. "And if so, how much might he have spilled about *us?* About what he'd found out about us?"

When the answer came, it was in Joe's exact words. They appeared on the screen slowly, as dictated to Carlos.

"*I know I gave you a bum steer before, about Roscoe not being any threat to the living so early. But I've given this one a lot of thought, and I honestly think there's no cause for alarm. Being a hardened criminal in life, Roscoe would have a built-in reluctance to giving strangers too many details about his affairs. So I think our secret is safe. So far.*"

The boys were silent for a while. Then Wacko turned.

"One thing I'm still puzzled about is this. If Vinnie's astral body had left him, how come his physical body still behaved partly like Vinnie—still knew so much about the candy and the senator and stuff?"

"Yeah," said Buzz. "And if Malevs can take over a person's body when its astral body vacates it, why don't they take over corpses? I mean, you never hear of corpses coming to life like that."

The screen had started flickering even before Buzz had finished speaking.

"You guys are getting to sound just like Lester! . . . But, no—sorry, fellas. Those are questions that have been puzzling some of us, too, and we've figured it out this way. First, the astral body is not just the mind, the personality, of the body it lives in. It's a duplicate. It's invisible to you, but it's a very real, very strong duplicate of both the body and mind, or personality, or soul, or whatever you like to call it. You with me so far?"

Both boys nodded.

"OK. So when the astral body leaves home temporarily, because it strays or gets clobbered by a Malev, the living body is weakened, sure enough. But it doesn't always die. It can linger on, even though its astral duplicate has left it. You still with me?"

"Sure," murmured Buzz.

"Go on," said Wacko.

"Well, it's the same with the personality, or mind, or inner ghost. Some weakened form of that stays behind, too. With all its memories and associations. All weakened, but still usable. Which is why, when a Malev takes over, he doesn't have only the body to work with. He has its memory and stuff, too. Like taking over an abandoned tank. You not only get the armor and weapons and engine, you get its communications system as well. A bit patchy, in this case, and with reduced energy input, but serviceable. Very, very serviceable for a short kamikaze run—especially that part of the system programmed for launching attacks, the aggressive part, the hating part."

"Yes," murmured Wacko. "I see. That explains why in all cases of possession I've heard about, the victim still has an idea where he is, and who his relatives and friends are."

"And his enemies!" said Buzz. He winced slightly.

"I still think it's too bad you didn't tell us all this earlier."

"Come on! We're not gods. We don't know everything just because we're ghosts. Only dummies think that. We can only go by what we observe, just like you. But you'd better believe that from now on, I, Carlos Gomez, for one, will be taking a very special interest in any astral bodies, any temporary ghosts, that we come across. Not that that will solve everything about them, either."

"Oh?" Buzz glanced up at the space in front of the word processor, rather anxiously. "What d'you mean?"

"Well, you just have to remember that in matters like this, the more you find out, the more you're made to realize that there are more and more mysteries still to be solved—mysteries and problems you'd never even dreamed of. Solve one, and you uncover a whole 'nother bunch. And so on."

"Yeah," said Wacko, staring thoughtfully at the word processor. "There's always another enigma."

"Complete with more surprises," said Buzz, with a grunt. "Not necessarily the pleasant kind, either!"

The ghosts had been wrong about one point in the report, however. The boys did hear from Detective Grogan, a few days later, on their way out of school. His car was parked in the yard, between the main door and the row of buses. He was apparently taking no chances on missing them.

"Get in," he said, reaching back and opening the rear door. "I'll give you a ride home."

They looked at each other before responding. This was no accidental meeting, obviously. On the other hand, it wasn't exactly official. They knew the detective well enough by now to realize that when he wanted an off-the-record but important discussion, he chose to hold it well away from the office—or any other place where they might be overheard.

When they stepped inside, Grogan got right down to business.

"I suppose you know you could have been killed?" he said, starting the car.

"Yes, sir," said Buzz.

"Both of you. The state he was in, he could have killed you both, single-handed."

"Yes, sir," said Wacko. "It was a good thing you came to the party, after all."

The detective grunted. He gave Wacko a sour look through the rearview mirror.

"Yes! Me and a few others . . . Which reminds me. I've been talking to Dino Gorusso."

The boys stirred uneasily.

"Sir?"

"And Dino Gorusso knows better than to withhold the names of informants in a case like this."

Neither boy knew what to say to that. The eyes in the mirror had an almost amused glint in them now.

"He tells me," the detective went on, "that some friends of yours saw the actual spiking being done. They were leaf raking or something, up at the senator's place. You want to tell me who they were *now?*"

Wacko gave Buzz a nudge, to let his friend know that *he* would do the talking at this point.

"Why?" said the lawyer's son. "Is Vinnie going to be charged, after all? Is there going to be an indictment?"

The cop's tight lips twitched in a smile.

"You know he isn't! The guy's very sick. . . . And nobody got hurt."

"But the attempt," said Wacko, pressing home his small victory. "The needles. A case could be made—"

"The guy wasn't in his right mind!" the detective snapped. "That's what the doctors say, anyway."

"But he made his threats in public," said Wacko, beginning to enjoy himself at Grogan's expense. "He made them in front of the TV people. *They* might want this thing to be taken further. You know what the media's like."

"He made those threats only in passing. A few crazy words as he went for Phillips here with a deadly weapon. Those people wouldn't be paying much attention to *words*, believe me. Even I wasn't. Except for something he said that—" Grogan broke off. Maybe it was so he could concentrate better on passing a pickup truck. Maybe not. A troubled, perplexed look had come into those eyes for a second or two. "Anyway," he said, having passed the truck, "speaking of needles, let's stick to the point. Who *were* those people who told you what they'd seen?"

Buzz shook his head.

"Sorry, sir, But we can't say."

"Can't? or won't?"

"It doesn't matter now, anyway," said Wacko. "Since there aren't going to be any charges."

Grogan nodded, then sighed.

"Let's just say I'm curious. Let's say I probably saved your lives up there, and it would be one way of thanking me."

The two boys squirmed a little. The detective had scored a hit there, all right!

"Well, yes, sir," said Wacko. "At least you saved us from some nasty injuries. And we *are* grateful."

"Yes, sir," said Buzz. "Thank you. Sincerely."

"So—the informants? Are you still sticking to—well—hunches, inspired guesses, psychic messages—that kind of thing?"

"Yes, sir!" said Buzz. "Because it's the truth!"

Buzz's face had flushed—but with a feeling of relief that it *was* the truth. Righteous relief.

The detective's eyes had been studying his reaction.

"I believe you," he said quietly.

This surprised Wacko.

"Sir?"

"I believe you," Grogan repeated. Then his voice took on a sharper edge. "I believe you've hit on some cockamamy, updated system of foretelling the future. Like they used to use playing cards, crystal balls, Ouija boards or whatever. Only you—*you're* using electronics."

That made them both gasp.

"Sure!" said the detective. "It's beginning to make sense to me. *You're* the computer whiz, aren't you?" The eyes flicked to Wacko. "Well, what I think is this. You've worked out some kind of program to feed into the computer your hunches or guesses and maybe a few scraps of facts. And then the machine takes over—works out the percentages, probabilities, possibilities—and finally comes up with some sort of a straight answer."

"Well . . . maybe—"

"It's OK, son. I don't want to steal your ideas. Because why? Because I don't believe in computers telling what's going to happen, any more than I believe in fairies, or goblins, or werewolves, or vampires, or—or ghosts."

Wacko fought to keep the relief out of *his* voice—to keep the whole discussion cool and scientific.

"There *has* been some very interesting research done on the subject," he said.

"Sure! And there have been a few interesting results. Wasn't this one of them? But it all comes back to chance and coincidence. Computers just narrow the percentages, cut down the odds of getting the answer wrong. But there are still a whole lot more wrong answers than right ones. It's like gambling. No matter how scientific a gambler's system is, there are more losing numbers than winners."

"Well, that's true, but—"

"I know it's true. I come across too many gamblers in my job to believe otherwise. . . . But here's where I have to give you guys a warning. When gamblers' predictions go wrong, they just lose their money. If *yours* go wrong—it could be more than that that you lose."

"Yes, sir."

"So just don't meddle. Enjoy your hobby. They tell me there's a great future in electronics, so stick to that. Leave the police work to us."

The car had come to a stop at an intersection not far from the boys' homes.

"OK?" said the cop, as they got out.

"Sure," said Buzz. "Thanks for the ride."

"It's what we do, anyway," said Wacko, watching

the car move off. "We always leave the police work to him. When he decides to *listen!*"

Buzz grinned.

"I must say he's getting mellower. He may not believe us one hundred percent, but—"

"No!" said Wacko, alarmed. "And we don't want him to, either. If he ever finds out the real truth, we'd all be in trouble. The biggest trouble yet!"

Three flicks on the right ear of each boy made them jump, then laugh.

"You can say that again!" was the obvious message.

There'd been eavesdroppers at Detective Grogan's unofficial off-the-record meeting, after all!